INVITATION TO DIE

INVITATION TO DIE

TO DIE

Helen Smith

THOMAS & MERCER

Text copyright © 2013 Helen Smith
Originally published as a Kindle Serial, March 2013

Published by Thomas & Mercer

PO Box 400818
Las Vegas, NV 89140

ISBN-13: 9781477807309
ISBN-10: 1477807306
Library of Congress Control Number: 2013902945

For Damon and Lauren

CHAPTER ONE
PRELIMINARIES TO MURDER

In Hartford, Connecticut, in the United States of America, just after eleven o'clock in the morning on a Saturday, Winnie Kraster received an invitation to die. Not realizing what it was, she accepted eagerly.

Winnie usually checked her email inbox several times a day at the weekend, even though her husband, Des, disapproved of what he called her "computering." That morning, as she scrolled down the list of messages, opening her correspondence and then deleting or responding as appropriate, her gorgeous Maine coon cat, Frederick, rubbed his leonine face against her leg. He put his front two paws onto her lap, in preparation to leap.

"Honey, no!" Winnie batted him away—he was distracting her, and she had nearly deleted it! But there it was: the email that was to change her life (though not, unfortunately, in a good way). The subject line of the email announced that she was a competition winner.

Normally, any email announcing amazing good news—a lottery win in Italy, for a lottery she had never entered, or money that was to be gifted to her by an official in Lagos in return for an administration fee—went straight into the trash folder on her computer. But this email was a genuine one. Winnie was thrilled to think that it would have reached her all the way from England only seconds after it had been sent, in the magical twinkle of time that cyber communications permit. This was the email that would validate all Winnie's hopes and dreams. This was the email that said, "Don't give up, girl! You've done it! You're worth something." It had been sent to her by the Romance Writers of Great Britain, a small but prestigious organization that claimed world-famous writers like Polly Penham and Morgana Blakely among its membership.

Winnie called to her husband, "Honey, get in here! You gotta see this!" There was no question of consulting him about how she should respond to the email from Morgana Blakely, president of the committee organizing this year's RWGB conference in London. Morgana had invited her to travel to London. Winnie would be there.

Winnie had a job as an administrator in an insurance company where Des also worked (it was where they had met, in fact, seven years ago). She spent all day in the office, but then she came home and spent several hours a night tending the blog that she wrote, as keenly as any gardener cultivating roses for a championship competition. If Des could have touched or held the results of her efforts, he might have been more interested. All he saw was his wife hunched over her computer—there was something miserly about it: the glow of the screen on her watchful face, the loneliness of it—as she uploaded reviews of romance novels she had read, and posted details of competitions that she or her readers might want to enter, and shared with her readers the difficulties she encountered as she tried to break into the market herself as a new writer.

Fortunately Des cared so little about Winnie's blog—written as Tallulah, under the blog name Tallulah's Treasures—that he rarely read it, and so he missed the posts where Winnie complained about some of the trivial but irritating details of their domestic life, sometimes even going so far as to suggest that she'd be happier if she could just stay home and write, with Frederick close by for comfort. And smoke! Yes, Des disapproved of his wife's sneaky cigarette habit. But she felt that nicotine helped her connect her thoughts sometimes.

Didn't the writer Winnie most admired in all the world, Polly Pen- ham, confess to treating herself to a cigarette from time to time to help the writing flow, as she polished off yet another funny, clever, adorable romantic comedy? Polly's books featured likeable yet ditzy young women whose antics could make Winnie laugh aloud as she sat and read them late at night in bed, Des grumbling at her side. Maybe Polly's next book would feature an American blogger with a Maine coon cat—Winnie could but hope.

Des understood how much his wife's dreams of getting pub- lished meant to her, even if he was sometimes jealous of the time she spent on her writing. If he was honest with himself (not with her—that would have been a mistake), he had just never thought it would come to anything. Now it seemed that her efforts had been validated. He came and stood behind her, one hand on her shoul- der, and read the email that was open on her screen:

```
TO: Winnie@TallulahsTreasures.com
FROM: Morgana@MorganaBlakely.co.uk
SUBJECT: Winning Writer in Our Online
Competition

Dear Winnie,

Thank you for submitting a romantic scene
to our online competition. Entries came
flooding in from around the world, and the
standard was very high. We're delighted
to tell you that our judging panel—
which included the organizing committee
of the RWGB conference, and the award-
winning writer Polly Penham—thought your
contribution was outstanding.
```

You have been chosen as one of the winning writers in our competition. Congratulations, Winnie! We would like to invite you to come to London to meet my agent, Lex Millington, of Millington Bussell, for afternoon tea and a chat about the publishing business at this year's Romance Writers of Great Britain conference, which will be held at the Coram Hotel in Bloomsbury, London.

After tea with Lex, Polly Penham will meet you and the other winning writers to share tips about her success. Later, we will get together with members of RWGB and guests from the industry for a gala dinner at the hotel. Your accommodation costs will be met for the night of the dinner.

Please let me know if you are able to attend. And, once again, congratulations!

Morgana

Des noted that the email promised very little other than "chats" with various people. Even the airfare wasn't included, from what he could see. But for Winnie this was to be the start of everything. She was overcome with happiness. Des bent and hugged his wife. He could feel her trembling as he put his arms around her. Whatever happened—even if this was to be another disappointment shared with readers on the Tallulah's Treasures blog—Des was determined that they would celebrate. He went to look in the kitchen to see if they had any white wine he could chill in the fridge. Maybe they could invite some friends over for barbecue tonight.

Winnie pulled the cuff of her sweater down past her right wrist and over the heel of her hand, and wiped her eyes with it. She took a couple of calming, slightly shuddery breaths. Then she began to compose an email accepting the invitation to go to London. She thought it was the beginning of everything. Des, out in the kitchen, a pack of lamb chops held to his nose to try to detect whether the meat was still fresh enough to serve to guests, was not so sure. He thought he might try to take a few moments later on to downgrade her expectations, even knowing that it might make her angry with him if he tackled the subject, with all the tactlessness of a long-married husband who cares too much to lie to his wife. It did make her angry. Unfortunately—though he would later wish for it over and over—Winnie would not live to hear Des say to her, "I told you so."

Cerys Pugh was getting her roots done at home in Cardiff, South Wales, in the United Kingdom. She was fortunate enough to know a hairdresser who would come to her house with all the equipment necessary, and charge a very reasonable price. Cerys was a writer and she worked hard at her job, and she liked to spend as little time as possible on distractions during the day. Even while Pam, the hairdresser, was attending to the dark pathways of Cerys's elegant silver-blonde bob, Cerys had her fancy phone in her hand, checking her emails.

"This phone," Cerys was fond of saying, "is my life. Photos and facts at your fingertips. Won't answer back. Won't get drunk at parties and demand that you drive it home. Won't go to the pub and want its dinner cooking in the meantime. What's not to like? If I could marry this piece of kit, I would." All of which reflected rather badly on Cerys's ex-husband, a mild-mannered man who had stayed in more often than he went out, and who could cook a very good lasagne, and who earned a decent living working for the gas board. The couple had had what Cerys called "our differences," and they certainly had different temperaments—Cerys was explosive and quick to blame, her ex slightly prone to depression, which could make him seem dull. But it did seem a bit harsh to compare him unfavorably to a phone.

Cerys and Pam chatted for a while about technology, men, grandchildren and the like. And then Cerys said, "I picked up something nasty on the Google Alert last week."

Pam was a creative individual who worked with her hands and rarely used a computer—though both her teenage sons had laptops at home—and at first she thought that Cerys was confessing to having a communicable disease. She couldn't continue with the appointment, if so—the risk of passing something on to other clients was too great. Pam had disposable gloves on her hands to protect her from the hair dye, and the strength of peroxide she used in it was likely to kill most germs. But even so...

"Goobie what?" said Pam, nervously. She paused in her work with her hands held up, about half a foot from Cerys's head, and slightly above it, as if preparing to contain invisible, toxic rays if they should leak out from Cerys's brain.

Whether she guessed what was going through Pam's mind, or she was just determined to get her point across about how nasty this thing was, Cerys held up her phone to show Pam that she was talking about an article she had found on the Internet. Pam bent, squinting a bit to try to see what this was all about—she'd needed reading glasses since she'd turned forty, but hairdressing was long-range, and her glasses weren't perched on her nose.

Cerys explained, "I set up an automated search on the Internet—see, Pam? Every week I get an email with a roundup of any mentions of my name or the title of any of my books. That way I can keep in touch with my fans and thank anyone who's left a review."

Pam wondered if calling her readers "fans" wasn't a bit self-indulgent. Cerys, God love her, wasn't Shirley Bassey. Still, we're all allowed our foibles. "That's nice," said Pam. Scare over, she continued with the application of the hair dye, wrapping the precut silver foil squares around segments of her client's hair, her fingers quick and sure, like an old-timer rolling cigarettes in front of a novice smoker.

"It *would* be nice, except that people don't have the manners they were born with, never mind what their mams taught them and what they learned in school." Cerys touched the screen a few times and then proffered the phone again. "Tell me what you think of this, Pam."

Pam bent again to look. She didn't at first understand the significance of what she was reading—you can't keep up with everything your clients produce, otherwise you'd go mad—so she didn't recognize the name of the book. But then she saw the name of the author: "Cerys Cadfael" (Cerys's pen name when she wrote historical fiction). From what Pam could see, someone on the Internet had written something horrid about Cerys's latest effort.

"Never mind, love," said Pam. "Don't worry about it."

Cerys took the phone back. "It's my baby, that book. That's how I feel. I've nurtured it into being, and now I watch over it as lovingly as any child, Pam."

Pam thought for a moment. She was used to playing the counselor for her clients—what hairdresser isn't? "Well," she said, "instead of a child, a living thing, why don't you think of it as something that your body's expelled? Does that help? Think of it as waste matter, Cerys. See what I'm saying? You've done it, now leave it. Get on with producing the next one."

Unfortunately, this didn't help. "You're not suggesting that my book—which took me the best part of a year to write: a product of my imagination, the blossoming flower of my passion—you're not suggesting, Pam, that I should look upon it as a great big poo?"

"Well…" Cerys was a regular client, and she tipped well. Pam backpedaled cautiously. "No, love, I don't suppose I am."

"It's my livelihood, and this woman is trashing it," said Cerys. She was still on about the review.

Pam wanted to move the conversation away from the subject of Cerys's livelihood and any potential threats to it, in case it prompted her client to reduce the tip she planned to leave. "Well, hopefully you'll never meet this woman. Least said, soonest mended, I always say."

"You're right," said Cerys. "You know me, Pam. I speak as I find. Good thing she lives in America. If I ever came face-to-face with her, I'd treat her to a few home truths."

"Does she now?" said Pam, impressed. "All the way in America, and she's read your book."

"She's kind to new writers, fair play to her. But heaven forbid you should get on her wrong side. Heaven forbid you should have established a reputation—never mind if you've worked tirelessly for twenty years to get to that point—and she gets it into her head you're getting too big for your boots."

"Is that what she said?" asked Pam. She hadn't taken in much of the review. She'd been too busy trying to understand its relevance to Cerys and why it was upsetting her to read the thing.

"Oh yes! And plenty more." Cerys read one of the choicer excerpts from the review: "'Cerys Cadfael is supposed to be taking her readers for a ride—you know the kind, where a rugged Celtic hero sweeps the heroine onto a white horse, gallops across the Welsh hills, and sweeps the heart of the reader along with the two of them. Oh, Ms. Cadfael takes her readers for a ride, all right; unfortunately, it's the wrong kind of ride, where someone coerces or cajoles you into paying a little more for something than you think it's worth.' The cheek of it, Pam! She didn't even pay for the book. 'Coerces or cajoles'! She was sent a free copy by my publisher, it's not like I'm taking the clothes off her kids' backs. And how do you like 'Ms. Cadfael'? So *proper*, while she gets her jabs in. It's not the *New York* bloomin' *Times*. Jealous—that's what she is."

"Well, never mind," said Pam. "At least you'll know not to send her the next one. What's her name, love?"

"Tallulah," said Cerys. "Ms. highfalutin Tallulah of Tallulah's Treasures, if you please."

◆　　◆　　◆

Nik Kovacevic had worked at the Coram Hotel in Bloomsbury in London for many years, but he had only recently been appointed to the position of general manager. What a prize! At thirty-two years of age, he'd made his mother proud. Unfortunately, this good news had caused resentment among some of his colleagues. Who was he, a former friend and confidant, to start giving them orders? Why had he been chosen over them anyway?

This morning Nik had gathered his heads of department together for what was to be the first of many briefing meetings. In common with management and administrative staff in hotels the world over, Nik wore a gray suit in imitation of a style of smart business dress that was rarely adopted these days by the hotel's guests. Like his colleagues, he wore a discreet name badge. At home, in front of the mirror, in suit and name badge, he had gone over his briefing speech several times, so as to be sure of making a good impression on his colleagues. In setting the tone for his tenure as general manager, he would be friendly yet firm. He would reassure colleagues that, as someone who was familiar with the Coram Hotel and the historical area in which it was located, he was a better choice than someone who might have been parachuted in by senior management to take charge. He was going to use the phrase "parachuted in" to make the point. In fact, his speech was to be peppered with jargon, which he hoped would impress everyone who heard it.

Once ensconced in the role, Nik was looking forward to worrying about personal performance targets and appraisals. He would mither over budgets. He would be properly anxious about illegal workers and Home Office raids. But, for now, the subject that most keenly absorbed him was the question of how to attract and retain foreign tourists—especially Americans—and how to persuade them to leave glowing reviews on travel booking sites.

"We are fortunate to operate in an area rich with history," Nik told his staff, as proudly as if he had created the history himself. The expressions on the faces of his staff ranged from a sullen *I know!* to a vacant *What are you talking about?* to a more gratifying *How fascinating*, from senior receptionist Miss Wendy Chen, who was new to the hotel.

Nik said, "What's our core business?"

There was a silence. There was no hostility in it, but neither was there any energy in the room. Nik smiled. He bounced on his feet to bring the energy up. He said, "That was a trick question! Conferences are very important to us. But so are American tourists. We have more than one core: what are we, an apple? No, indeed. This hotel is a honeycomb, full of worker bees!"

There was another silence. The speech had worked better at home in his bedroom, where Nik had even built in pauses for appreciative laughter and earnest questions, which he had acknowledged in the mirror with a gracious nod and a smile. He continued: "I want to see each and every one of you giving one hundred and ten percent when it comes to our conference delegates. And another hundred and ten percent for our American guests." Mathematics wasn't his strongest subject. But then he wasn't giving a lesson in percentages, he was trying to motivate his staff.

"What about Americans attending conferences?" asked someone, trying to catch him out.

"Well, it's quite simple. When you are dealing with American guests," said Nik, "whether their purpose in coming here is business or pleasure, you go the extra mile." He put his clenched fist just above shoulder height, as if he was about to walk that extra mile now. He was Dick Whittington on the road to London, off to make his fortune with his belongings in a handkerchief slung from a pole over his shoulder: a decent, honest man from humble beginnings who had risen to great power. Someone—Albin, one of the chefs—saw another amusing reference and sang, "Heigh-ho!"

Someone else joined in: "Heigh-ho!"

Nik knew what was going on. They resented his promotion. They weren't sure if they were going to take him seriously. They weren't sure if they were going to follow his orders. They were being impertinent, but in a way that would allow them to claim they were "only joking" or, "I thought we were friends, Nik" if he got cross about it or threatened to report them to Human Resources.

The chefs were a nightmare anyway. Now the TV was full of programs about celebrity chefs (when did chefs become the new rock stars, and more to the point, why?). The fryers and bakers in his kitchen thought of themselves as artistes: Picasso with a pickle. They were weasels, the lot of them.

His staff were staring: bored, amused or bewildered. Dry mouthed, Nik looked around for inspiration, trying to remember the thread of his speech. Weasels…Dick Whittington…Disney… Oh yes! That was it: Americans. A sense of desperation now urged him into fanciful rhetoric. Departing from his carefully rehearsed speech, he said, "Let's say our American guests are cold: let them know you'd do anything to warm them. You'd fetch them a blanket, you'd hand over your jacket, you'd…you'd peel off a layer of *skin* and drape it over them." He had the attention of the room now. Wendy Chen shuddered.

Nik bit his fingers anxiously. He hated this job. No! He loved it. It would settle down. They'd come to respect him. He'd do well here. The big bosses—the management of the hotel chain— would see it and promote him to another hotel, where he'd never have to see any of these idiots again. A settling-in period was inevitable. It would be worth it, if he could just deal with the stress of the next few weeks, and keep it together, and make sure nothing went wrong.

He decided to explain about his proposed austerity measures, which he hoped would earn him the attention of senior management.

"There's too much waste. Let's squash the waste! I'm going to make it my personal responsibility to check all the waste."

Nik suspected that staff took the odd steak home, leftover fruit, maybe. That was fine. It was the stuff that wasn't really leftover, the stuff that got pinched, that Nik was worried about. If they knew he was watching them and measuring what got thrown away, they wouldn't be so quick to smuggle food out of the hotel that was un-accounted for.

"We're going to do this across every department of the hotel. I'll be checking the wastage of everything from cabbages to toilet paper to printer paper. It doesn't just save money. It helps the environment. The Coram's going green! Look, I know this isn't going to be easy at first. At the end of each month we'll name a Rubbish Champion. That Rubbish Champion's photograph will appear on the staff noticeboard in my office, and they will get a Marks & Spencer voucher worth twenty-five pounds."

Everyone looked unimpressed. Never mind. As Nik prepared to close the meeting, he had a brilliant idea. He would turn the insubordination of the chef to his advantage. When you are a senior manager, it doesn't matter if something goes wrong—things always go wrong. What's important is how you deal with that situation. Nik would show that he was the master of it. He clenched his fist again, now pretending to shoulder a work tool, and he sang, "Heigh-ho!" This would be a rallying call; a fun way to end all their briefing meetings, with everyone joining in and...But, sensing it was over and the meeting was breaking up, everyone rushed for the door, anxious to get to work and meet their targets, and stop being told how to do a job they knew how to do. No one joined in singing.

When the last person had left, Nik closed the door and got out the work sheets for the next week, to familiarize himself with them and anticipate any potential "situations." It looked as though it would be rather a sedate week: the usual tourists, restaurant bookings and midweek business guests, and—of course—there was the conference of romance novelists. Very refined. Nothing to worry about there.

◆　◆　◆

TO: Mcrowther@cam.ac.uk
FROM: Morgana@MorganaBlakely.co.uk
SUBJECT: Next weekend

Muriel,

Can you let me know the title of the ethics in literature session you're doing for us at the conference next weekend? I think you said it would be something along the lines of "Why Does It Matter if I'm Making It Up?" I need to get it right for the program.

I'm so glad you're joining us. Your ideas are always so stimulating and clever, and amusing too, which is very important because we'll be cloistered in a series of windowless rooms all day. Do come for the gala dinner on Saturday night, won't you? I've got Lex coming, and you two always amuse each other. Publishing people have a terrible habit of talking shop, and Lex has been doing that for nearly forty years, and it bores him. So if you'll come to dinner, I'll put you next to him if you don't mind.

I'm going to need some support on the admin side. Do you know anyone who might be free to help out? We can pay reasonably well, and we'll put them up in the hotel and feed them (you too, of course, unless you'd rather go home after the dinner). It's going to be one of those weeks. I need someone at my side who will make things better, not worse. There are so few of those kinds of people around these

days. Let me know if you get any bright
ideas.

See you then,
M x

P.S. How is your hip? Any better? I do
hope so! I'm looking forward to a proper
catch-up and a lot of fun—if I can get
through the committee meeting without
throttling anyone.

◆　◆　◆

"Emily? Emily Castles?" The voice on the phone sounded like
menthol cigarettes and feathers. "I don't know if you'd remember
me..."

But Emily knew instantly who was calling. No one else had
a voice quite like Morgana Blakely, the famous romance novelist,
whom Emily had met while helping out at a local stage school.

"I'm presiding over a gathering of romance authors at a conference in London this weekend."

Surely there was a more appropriate word than gathering: a
pash, a kiss, a *smooch* of romance authors?

Morgana interrupted Emily's mental thesaurusing. "I rather
think I've overfaced myself, and I need a hand with it. Muriel put
your name forward. Would you be free to help, by any chance?"

Emily was free, as it happened. Until last Friday she had been
working on a temporary contract in a tower in the financial district
of Canary Wharf, East London. The tower was shiny, imposing and
soulless. It was the sort of place where the occupants of a crowded

elevator never asked incomers which floor they wanted, so that someone near the relevant buttons could press the one that would take everyone to their respective destinations: they expected you to push and stretch to get to the button yourself. Emily had tried calling out, "Forty-five, please!" She had tried shouting, "Which floor?" if she herself had managed to get nearer the operating panel than the other people piling into the elevator. Her words were met with resistance or incomprehension. After a few days she had realized that if you wanted to change the world, an elevator in a tower in Canary Wharf might not be the best place to start. It had depressed her, but at least she'd had the money to pay her phone bill at the end of the month.

The people in the department where she had been "embedded" (according to the bizarre new terminology from her handler at the employment agency, who persisted in talking as though Emily were a reporter dispatched to a faraway war) had been friendly enough, but the work had not been satisfying. Still, Emily had been sorry that the contract had come to an end. She would be glad of any kind of employment, even a weekend at a gathering of romance authors. Well, *especially* a weekend at a gathering of romance authors—depending on her duties, of course.

"All you have to do," Morgana explained, "is turn up tomorrow morning at the Coram Hotel in Bloomsbury so we can get the delegates' gift bags organized, and then be on hand for the gala dinner and the conference itself. I'm so glad you can help out. I was so impressed with your resourcefulness when we met. And, of course, Muriel speaks very highly of you." Muriel was "Dr. Muriel" to Emily; a neighbor who lived on the same street as Emily in South London, as did Morgana's nephew, Piers Blakely, and his wife, Victoria.

Emily wasn't the sort of person to wonder whether Piers spoke very highly of her as well. He always offered her a glass or two of chilled white wine when the family was about to go on holiday, and Emily went round to be briefed about how best to look after their cat. If Piers kept his opinion of Emily to himself when talking to Morgana—even if it was a good opinion—so much the better. As for Victoria, she was indebted to Emily for Emily's intervention during the end-of-term show at the stage school she owned and ran, which was where Emily had first met Morgana. Emily had saved lives at that show. She didn't doubt that Victoria spoke very highly of her indeed.

"When the conference gets underway," Morgana said, "I'd be grateful if you'd take notes during the speeches and debates—I'm chairing 'Whither the Novel?' again this year—and liaise with the hotel staff. Do you know how to spell 'liaise'?"

"I do," said Emily. "Two i's."

"Darling, I'm so glad you're on board. You're so clever and literate. One word of warning: if anyone talent-spots you and asks you to ghost one of their novels, do say no. They don't pay very well. And if anyone asks you to do *anything* when they're drunk, just say yes, but don't do it. They ask for such silly things. And if anyone asks you to do anything when *you're* drunk, well...How old are you?"

"Twenty-six," said Emily.

"That's old enough. But we've got some of the chaps coming in from the various publishing houses tomorrow. One or two of them find female company overstimulating. They look around the room and they see pretty hair and ready smiles and they think they're in a Lynx advert and behave accordingly. Do you know what Lynx is?"

"Isn't it a deodorant marketed to teenage boys?"

"I give it to Piers and Victoria's eldest every Christmas to keep the girls away. I hope you never have to smell it, Emily. You can find the address of the hotel on the Internet, can't you? See you at midday tomorrow."

◆ ◆ ◆

In the gray, historic city of Edinburgh, in Scotland, Archie Mears opened his notebook and took the lid off his pen. He was a slim man in his midthirties, with very pale skin and thick, blood-orange hair that flopped forward as he looked down at the page in front of him, accentuating the sharpness of his high cheekbones.

It was early morning, and hardly anyone or anything except the drunks and the pigeons were up and about. Archie's former life—the one he didn't discuss with anyone, even close family—had got him into the habit of rising early. He would start today, as he started every day, with twenty minutes of automatic writing, following a set of rules he had learned at the creative writing workshop where he had met Morgana Blakely. When he wrote like this, he didn't think. He put pen to paper and he just wrote, so that the process seemed unconnected to him, almost magical. Gradually, in the writing, there emerged fragments of the previous night's dreams, remembered as best he could, segueing into an acknowledgment of some of his hopes and fears. His fears were of being trapped by fire or water—of being hurt, physically. Were these snippets dreams or daydreams? They were sometimes violent: He was a little boy, lashing out at his parents. He was an angry man, challenging authority. And then came the soothing idea of a happy-ever-after: the favorite part of a story he had read or written, or one he was working on, would present itself on the page. As he wrote the happy-ever-after, he would begin to feel calm. It was a kind of meditation for him—going over and over the same things, finding something slightly different in them each time, being soothed by them each time.

Archie took his notebook with him whenever he left home. The ritual of writing in it calmed him and prepared him for the day, though he rarely looked back over it. It was not a way of making plans or generating ideas. He only wanted to spill the thoughts and then move on. Other than the happy endings, the content was dark and disturbing, a jumble of nonsense punctuated by violent images. There were the shape-shifting, half-remembered, initially rather mundane situations of his dreams: *I was walking down the road and I saw Sheena, and then I realized it was Sookie, and we were supposed to go to the shop on the corner because we hadn't any milk for our tea.* Then the memory or the imagination burrowed down another layer and uncovered something nastier. There were children's dirty faces barely glimpsed at an upstairs window as flames engulfed a house. There were violent blows from a man's big fist. There were screams, cries, a woman pleading for help. There was not enough food. There were babies with nappy rash, their neglected little bottoms soaked in urine. There were attempts to escape, and hands hauling the woman back. On some pages in the notebook there was a throat cut in the night, though on other pages there were descriptions of violent dogs let out of a locked room, doing damage to human flesh with their slobbery, sharp teeth. Sometimes angels or demons were released, and they swooped down and crushed the man, though he fought back violently.

These tormented fragments were followed with longer passages about romantic love that were expressed more coherently, if a little tritely, revealing characters and stories that would be familiar to readers of the popular romance novels that Archie wrote and published under the name of Annie Farrow. These books usually featured a kind, strong man intervening to save a long-suffering woman and reward her travails by offering her a second chance in life. The kind man would be unassuming; she wouldn't notice him at first, thinking that there was no hope, that no one would intervene to prevent her humiliation at the hands of the violent brute she had married. She would be hardworking, from a low social class, not beautiful but with an inner purity that outsiders sensed and appreciated. She would be almost broken by her troubles. But this kind man would have the courage and the finances to be able to whisk her away—taking her small children with them, if she had any—to start a new life with him a long, long way away, in Canada or Australia or America, or sometimes in the Scottish Highlands. The new life would be tough but rewarding. She would learn to love the kind man. She would forget the other.

Page after page of Archie's notebook went like this: mundane situations, misremembered fragments, horrible images of a woman and children suffering, retribution, and then the happy-ever-after with a decent life with a kind, loving man, in a land far, far away.

Outside in Edinburgh, in a street silvered with rain, a taxi tooted its horn. Archie went to the window and looked down. The taxi was waiting for him. He closed the notebook. He put the lid back on his pen. He put it, with the notebook, into his hand luggage. The contents of such a notebook might be difficult to explain if the book should fall into insensitive hands. Not everyone believes in the happy-ever-after. There is a certain kind of reader who would be disinclined to try to interpret the dream sequences as dreams, who might concentrate on the horrible images of carving, cutting, stabbing, biting and fighting. To such a person—a policeman, perhaps—Archie's morning scribblings would be a sign of a disturbed mind, perhaps describing some kind of sick fantasy that he wanted to carry out.

Below, the taxi tooted its horn again. Archie looped the handle of his hand luggage over the metal pull-along handle of his modest-size suitcase. He took a quick look round the flat to make sure everything was switched off that ought to be off, and all the windows closed. He patted his pockets—wallet, keys, a small amount of loose change. He had everything he needed. He went downstairs to get into the taxi. It was to take him to the station where he would catch a train to King's Cross in London, traveling on from there by taxi to the Coram Hotel in Bloomsbury.

◆　　◆　　◆

Monsieur Cyril Loman sat on a wooden stool behind the counter of his confectionery shop in a Regency Arcade off Piccadilly in London, and read the *Daily Mail.* It was quite early in the morning, and there were no customers in his shop. If there had been, he would have been standing, politely waiting for an inquiry, ready to be of service. This shop was his pride. It was a good business. As well as what was available to passing trade on glass shelves in the shop, M. Loman also supplied hotels, embassies and wealthy private individuals. With enough notice, he could make for your child's birthday a teddy bears' picnic created with chocolate bears, and all the fruits in the picnic basket—even the basket itself—made from confectionery. He would remember your wife's birthday, your mistress's birthday, your mother's birthday, your personal assistant's birthday, your boss's birthday, your children's birthdays, your wedding anniversary, even when you were too busy to remember these dates yourself. He could make a filling for a chocolate that was as individual and intimate as a perfume on a woman's skin. His chocolates told a story. They asked you to remember the taste of summer when you were a child, or the kiss of a woman you loved when you were nineteen years old. They whispered memories of a holiday with your lover in France, or Christmas with the family at home.

With his chocolates, M. Loman created and sold fantasies— even to himself. He found a little fantasy was necessary to get through each day because, up until the age of fifteen, when he reached this country after several failed attempts and was finally able to claim political asylum, he had had a very difficult life.

Even now, granted leave to remain in the UK and with a long apprenticeship at his craft, followed by longer years as a successful businessman, life was not easy. M. Loman read the English newspapers and worried. The articles complained of illegal immigrants and overcrowding. M. Loman had the sense of something closing in. The tax on luxury goods had increased, making his chocolates slightly less attractive to customers than they had been the previous year. There were peaks in sales. Valentine's, of course, was a good time for purveyors of chocolates. He wished the world were more romantic. French is one of several languages he speaks. The English, so proud of their fair-mindedness, so self-deprecating about their plodding kindness, were in fact very quick to judge. And mean with money. Why not splash out on treats? All they had going for them was their National Health Service, and they were quietly dismantling that. He had suffered horribly in his past. The things he had seen…Mostly he wanted to forget, but he couldn't forget. Talking helped. Helping others helped. And he had treatment for the injuries to his body from caring professionals. M. Loman paid his taxes and national insurance like everyone else, and was a regular visitor to the outpatient clinic near his home.

The business he ran involved catering to pampered, rich people who had no idea what it was like to try to balance the books every day. He wished he could say that none of them had any idea what he himself had endured, so far away, so long ago. But sometimes he saw someone, an exile from a corrupt regime, or even a current participant in it, and there was something in their eyes—not cruelty so much as *knowing*. They knew there was evil in the world because they had witnessed it or participated in it. They came into the shop and bought bonbons for pretty daughters, or they got out their credit card to pay for a chocolate unicorn ordered by a mistress for an extravagant party, and they looked at Cyril Loman and he looked at them, and they both *knew*. They were in a chocolate shop in an ornate historical covered arcade in Piccadilly. Green Park was in front of them, Hyde Park was just over there. Buckingham Palace was a short walk away in one direction, Fortnum & Mason in the other. Mayfair was behind them. The law was all around them. Fresh air and calm green spaces, shopkeeping, the British legal system—all these things were prized both by the British public and Cyril Loman. It (as well as his admiration for the NHS) was what had persuaded him to make his home here—at great expense; his family had spent everything on his passage here, and there was no safety net. But, in the end, it might not be enough to protect him. Those bullies with the knowing eyes knew it. They looked at him as they bought their bonbons for their pretty daughters and sometimes—choosing at random a half-pound box of chocolate-covered bitter orange sticks, or chocolate-covered maraschino cherries—they said, "Give me one of those, as well." And M. Loman smiled and added it to the order, knowing they didn't intend to pay for it. They stood there, in their expensive suits that had been tailored to fit their big, greedy bodies, and they took a pound of chocolates without paying for them, because it was all M. Loman had to give, and because they could. Were they suggesting, by doing it, that they suspected M. Loman had not got here strictly legally? That, though he dutifully paid his taxes and his national insurance on behalf of Cyril Loman, they suspected Cyril Loman might be surprised to know it, having died prematurely around twenty years ago. M. Loman was a man whose shop stood, metaphorically speaking, on quicksand. He was not surprised when he felt his feet sink half an inch or so into the cold mud below him, and he knew it was best not to struggle or he would just go deeper in. But if it came to it, he would throw a rope around something or someone to pull himself out, and if they should fall in beside him, he couldn't promise that he wouldn't step on their shoulders to get himself out. Because wherever M. Loman came from—was it the Democratic Republic of the Congo? Was it Haiti? Was it Rwanda?—he had no intention of going back.

The doorbell jangled, and M. Loman put the newspaper down and leaped lightly to his feet. The customer was one he recognized and was cautiously fond of. A slightly eccentric, elfin woman in a blue angora beret who stretched out both hands to him (rather awkward—a handshake was more businesslike, the two-hand grasp implied that one of them had just won a BAFTA, and that wasn't ever going to happen).

"Monsieur Loman," she said, in her smoky Marianne Faithfull voice, "I have the most marvelous sponsorship opportunity for you. Are you busy now? Can we talk about it?"

M. Loman knew what this meant. This lovely lady, who lived in material comfort in her tidy little million-pound townhouse in Highgate, was not going to stiff him for a box of handmade chocolates. No indeed. She was going to stiff him for forty boxes. And he was going to pretend to be happy about it. Business was business. Something might come of it.

"Is it time for the conference already, Mizz Blakely?" he inquired. "How the days go by so fast." He took her two hands in his, bowed, and kissed them. He was the perfect French gentleman. The creator of fantasies.

◆　◆　◆

Zena was lying in the bath in her flat in Muswell Hill in North London. Not *lying* in it: she was luxuriating in it. Her fingers, with their purple-painted nails, hung loosely over each side of the enamel rim at the top of the bathtub, ensuring the skin stayed wrinkle-free. Her hands and her mind were perhaps the two most important parts of Zena, because they helped her to earn her living. She needed her fingers for typing, and she protected them from potentially damaging household chores, like cleaning and cooking. She didn't like to open so much as a can of tomatoes for fear of slicing her fingers and slowing her progress at the keyboards. Paper cuts were an unavoidable injury in her line of work, but she tried to avoid all other possible injuries to her hands, so far as she could. Her mind was to be treasured more than any physical part of her. She visualized it as a beautiful dove that nestled most of the time in a jeweled cathedral (the high domed ceiling of the cathedral was created by the bones of her skull; the jewels that decorated it were her brown tourmaline eyes and her pretty white teeth), but some days she sent the dove flying off beyond the physical limits of its existence by expanding her consciousness, then brought it home again bearing some magical gift for her in its beak. Zena was a person who was unembarrassed about thinking of herself as the center of the world, and being showered with gifts.

This morning the dove was still perched in its cathedral, its soft breast fluttering as it dreamed the stories that fed her imagination, while Zena's body swam safely in the waters of the warm, silky, scented artificial lake she had created within the porcelain shores of her bathtub in North London.

The bathwater covered most of Zena's body and all of her modesty. There were just the two dark brown islands of her knees above the milky sea that she lay in, and of course her neck, face and head, her hair hidden away beneath a puffy, purple bath hat.

Zena hummed. Why not? She was happy. It was midmorning and she was in the bath. It was part of her job to lie here and prepare herself to write her sensual stories. She was an indolent person, but when she thought of her preparations for her writing day, she compared herself to an athlete—in those few moments before a sprinting race when the fingertips touch the ground, when mind and body are in tune, and then—whoosh!—all the power of the body is unleashed. In her case, as she lay here, fingertips touched to the enamel of her bathtub, water cooling, she was preparing herself for the moments afterwards when her mind would be unleashed.

Zena liked to rehearse the events of the day in her mind before she carried them out. It was an exercise in positive thinking, but it also helped to reinforce her sense of herself as some kind of North London goddess: she imagined something, and then it came to pass. And, a little like the gods and goddesses of ancient mythology, if something didn't come to pass exactly as she had imagined it, she could sometimes be a little cranky, to say the least.

This morning, she imagined receiving a call on her mobile phone. And, lo, the phone started to ring. Of course, this was because Zena had booked a call with a local journalist. But in imagining it, she was prepared for it.

The voice on the line said, "Hiya! Zena? It's Trevor here. This a good time to talk?"

And Zena said, "Yes, baby. Ask me anything. Zena's ready for it!"

"Tell me about your day. What's in store for you?"

"Being a spiritual person, I usually spend an hour chanting in the morning."

"Football?" said Trevor, a little surprised. He wasn't a sports fan himself. But the rivalry between London teams was notorious: Arsenal and Tottenham Hotspur in North London, Chelsea and Fulham in the west, West Ham in the east, Millwall in the southeast. He wouldn't have pegged Zena for a footie fan, but if she was, presumably she favored Arsenal or Tottenham. He just couldn't imagine her chanting songs popular on the football terraces for an hour every morning, unless perhaps she did it to train her voice.

"It's part of my Buddhist practice, Trevor. Nuthink to do with football, you lemon. I chant to align the spiritual and the physical dimensions of my world."

"Oh, I see!" Trevor sounded relieved.

"I'm interested in nature. See, I have a keen sensibility for the influence of taste, touch, smell, sound and sight on my well-being. I put fresh flowers on the windowsills. I burn incense on the altar in my house. I'm drawn to certain colors, like gold and purple—empress colors. Knowing how much influence even the most fragile elements of the universe can have on me, I try to influence the universe—not just with words. There's more subtle ways. There's the chanting…"

"And the altar? You said you have an altar?"

Zena laughed. "You think I'm gonna tell you I practice black magic, yeah? Only a little *Zena* magic, bro. The lady's black but the magic isn't."

Trevor laughed, too. He was also black, so he didn't mind Zena kidding about the color of her skin—he knew she wasn't doing it to see if it made him uncomfortable, the way she might with a white journalist. Just so long as she kept off the subject of football, he could get through the interview without any awkwardness. He really didn't know anything at all about football.

"What do you worship on your altar?" he asked. "Do you use it for worship?"

"Say there's some element of your life, yeah, that needs acknowledgment or control? That's what it's for. So if there's something that

I want to celebrate or influence, I'll place it on the altar. I might put one of my books there, and be thankful that it's been published, and hope it'll do well with sales. Or I might put a little doll there that represents a person who's important to me. My grandma, say, when she was sick for a while."

"Oh yeah!" said Trevor. "Yeah, I can see why you'd do that." He almost sounded convinced. Like many nicely brought-up young men (and some of the bad boys too), Trevor loved his grandma.

"See what I'm saying! He's listening to Zena now," said Zena. She was all for speaking in the third person when the drama or emotion of a situation demanded it. "Yeah, but it doesn't have to be all about celebration, Trevor. See, right now, I'm trying to give up smoking cigarettes. So I put a cigarette butt in there, on my altar, and I ring the little silver bell I keep to the side, and then I crush the cigarette butt with my fingers; I peel off the paper and shred it; I mash up the nasty, sticky, brown filter. Symbolically, I'm crushing a very nasty habit. Yeah? And that prepares Zena to beat it in real life. So that's how I use my altar. Plus, when I light it, the incense smells nice."

Trevor laughed. She imagined him scribbling away, impressed, though he might actually just be recording this. Did he realize she was in the bath? It would only add to her allure, like the earthly goddess Cleopatra before her.

"I grew up a sassy North London girl, Trevor, with my share of setbacks. I'm not afraid to strike out at someone or something I believe is holding me back. Sure, Zena's a bold, beautiful, spiritual woman who has risen up in life, and she likes to help others rise up. I'm a mentor to wayward children, disaffected youth, disenfranchised adults and other writers."

"Me too, I'm a mentor to some kids in a local school. What is it about being black that means we've all got to be a beacon for our local community? You ever wish you could be frivolous, Zena, instead of being a saint?"

"You don't have to be a saint, brother. Someone wants to make an enemy of me? They better watch out. I can be a saint, but I can be vindictive, too."

"I bet you can," said Trevor. "Someone would have to be an idiot to make an enemy of you."

"You're right. Crush or be crushed, yeah? Ain't no one ever wants to know what it's like to be crushed by Zena."

"Unless in the most passionate, romantic sense," said Trevor, dutifully, offering Zena an opportunity to chat about her work (the real purpose of the call) and her new novel, a sensual romance called *Venus in Velvet*. Zena explained that she would be discussing the book during her appearance at the upcoming Romance Writers of Great Britain conference. She plugged a few other events—a book signing at a shop in Kensington, a reading at a spoken word event in Shoreditch—and made sure that Trevor was clear about where his readers could buy her books, both in store and online, and then they ended the call.

Zena stepped, finally, out of the bath, with the grandiosity of a rock star emerging from an onstage water feature to rapturous applause. She planted one foot onto the bath mat, then the other, her ten purple-painted toenails making a V-shape like migratory birds. She pulled off her purple shower cap and shook loose her plaited hair so that it tumbled almost to her shoulders. She patted the moisture off her skin with a towel, and then made a fair attempt to put a little back in by rubbing coconut body salve over herself. She hummed again. Almost everything she did was self-congratulatory, but then there was a lot that she had to be happy about, considering her past and what she had overcome. She was inspirational—many people had told her so: at the schools where she went to talk to excluded children, and the institutions where she went to talk to adults with difficult lives. She thought of herself as having a calming influence. But she was a big woman, and she could be physically intimidating. Her physical presence was one of the reasons she was listened to with respect by wayward children. They respected her powerful physique and the thrilling tales of all the awful things she had got up to at their age; they were slightly baffled when she started talking about doves and jewels and cathedrals.

Zena got dressed. Breakfast would be next—toasted crumpets with butter and honey on them, and a pot of sweetened mint tea. She used to finish breakfast by rolling herself a cigarette, lighting it and inhaling deeply on its calming smoke. But now she was a non-smoker. Instead she would take deep, calming breaths…

She put two crumpets in the toaster and set the timer. When they popped up with a promising ping, hot and crunchy, she slathered them with butter so that it would melt and dribble into the random, tiny holes on the surface of each. Then she took the lid off the jar of honey, dipped her knife in and scraped around. There was hardly any honey left in the jar—not enough to sustain a bee, let alone a big, busy black woman with cigarette cravings. Zena lived alone, there was no one to blame for having used the honey without buying a new jar to replace it, but she didn't feel she herself was at fault. She blamed the universe. She took the jar and flung it at the wall, where it shattered, leaving a sticky smear, and then fell tinkling onto the tiles of her kitchen floor. Her heart pounded and her breath came quickly. Being calm, being sensual, was hard work sometimes. The little dove in her head fluttered and pecked, anxiously. On days like this she wished she had a gun: she'd shoot the stupid thing and bake it in a pie.

Zena took a moment to calm herself and review how the day had gone so far (good and then not so good) and how it might go after this, and how it might go in the days to come. She was looking forward to getting to the conference, catching up with Morgana and the rest of the guys, room service, lots of pampering in the spa. Maybe what she needed was contact with humankind—with womankind. She had kept herself shut away for too long in her flat in North London. She hadn't realized it at first, but the shattering of that honey jar symbolized her shattered ego. The universe was trying to tell her that she suffered too much for her art.

For now, she could get herself back on track by chanting, and lighting the incense at her altar. When she'd agreed to answer questions from that journalist, she hadn't expected so much interest in her altar! More people should have them: hers was a very useful addition to her life. So useful, in fact, that she also had a small, portable version that she could take with her anywhere, with a tiny silver bell, an incense holder, and a place to put a miniature representative of whatever she sought to influence...or crush. She would be taking it with her to the conference in Bloomsbury. There was no telling when she might need powerful magic like that.

CHAPTER TWO
THE CORAM HOTEL

The day was drearily damp and gray when Emily arrived at the Co-ram Hotel in Bloomsbury. Her short, dark hair was neatly combed; her shoes were new but comfortable to stand in. She was wearing her best coat, and she was carrying a small case she had packed with the requisite amount of underwear, some smart clothes for the daytime and a flattering dress for dinner. The hotel was an enor-mous Gothic structure fashioned from salmon-colored bricks, the sky above it as gray as a slab of panfried tuna. From the street, it was impossible to tell what it would be like inside; it might be musty and mildewy, more hostel than hotel. But the salute from the el-egant doorman, who touched his right hand to the brim of his gray bowler hat as Emily arrived, hinted at lavish interiors and first-class service beyond the heavy door he held open for her. Emily felt her shoulders relax as she went through into the dark calm of the hotel, the cool air spicy with the perfume of long-stemmed lilies. This weekend was going to be as relaxing as a spa break—a much-needed antidote to the stress of working in the cutthroat environment of London's financial district.

Emily didn't think of herself as a fanciful person, but she some-times had fanciful thoughts. As she stepped through the doors into the immaculately artificial, recently restored lobby of the hotel—the furniture, carpets, mirrors, even the *air* apparently heavier and richer than anything anyone would have at home—Emily had an impression of unreality, as if she had stepped through a portal into a previous age. She looked out again at the mackerel-gray streets—at the present-day people striding past, heads down against the wind, their slightly bitter expressions suggesting they had expected the day to turn out better than this—and saw that the world was just as she had left it.

Emily saw Morgana waiting for her in the lobby with the hotel manager and went over to meet her. A badge on the lapel of his suit announced that the manager's name was Nik Kovacevic. He had been confiding to Morgana that he would like to write a book. People always did this when they got her alone for five minutes, so she was used to it. They made it perfectly clear that it was a lack of time, rather than a lack of talent, that was preventing them setting the publishing world alight, as if Morgana was some kind of laya-bout who sat around writing books because she had nothing better to do with her time.

"I'd like to write a book about this place," Nik said.

"What a brilliant idea. You must do it."

"The stories I could tell. I know where the bodies are buried! Is it difficult to get an agent?"

"I'll put you in touch with mine, if you like. Just let me know when you've finished your manuscript."

"They don't pay advances these days, then?"

"They do. But they like to see what you've written first."

"It's finding the time, isn't it?"

Morgana introduced Emily to Nik. He bowed deferentially in that English way that seems borderline mocking to other English people. "The staff at the Coram Hotel will take great pleasure in working with you to make this conference a success. My office is just behind Reception if you need anything." He bowed again and then withdrew.

Morgana was wearing a smart powder-blue, velveteen trouser suit, a fluffy blue angora beret atop her head. Silver bangles jingled on her wrists as she turned to give Emily a kiss on the cheek. With the jingling, and the soft, appealing jumble of textures she was wearing in blue, Emily thought that Morgana would have made an excellent educational toy for a baby. But irreverence and employment are not a good mix, so Emily tried to compose herself and think businesslike thoughts.

"Let me introduce you to the others," Morgana said, and turned and walked very fast through the hotel's opulent interior, Emily beside her. Emily looked to left and right, taking in glimpses of silk patterned wallpaper, silk-upholstered furniture, uniformed staff, tall vases, short tables, stopped clocks, and a gilt barometer, as Morgana briefed her about the conference and its attendees. And then they reached the mahogany-lined bar. It featured a ceiling-high mirror, its reflection doubling the range of wines and spirits available behind the well-stocked bar, and giving the white-shirted, French-looking bar steward a twin. She briefly saw her twin there too—short, dark, bobbed hair, freckles, dimples, an eager expression and a nice strong little chin. Beyond her own reflection, Emily saw Morgana's fellow committee members in the mirror before looking into the room and seeing them in real life. Three of them—two women and a man—sat at a low, round table in the hotel bar eating steak and horseradish sandwiches in crusty white bread, the bloody red juices from the meat running down their fingers as though they had just taken part in a ritual killing.

Morgana introduced each of them in turn. The first was Cerys, a big Welsh woman in her fifties with white-blonde hair cut into an expensive bob. Emily put out her hand in greeting. Cerys stood and picked up her napkin. The heavy rings on her fingers formed a solid mass, like a sparkly knuckle duster, as she curled her fingers around it. She put her shoulders back and pushed her chin forward just a few millimeters. She wiped her hands, very slowly. She didn't shake Emily's hand. "Are you one of the bloggers?" she said to Emily, distrustfully.

"Goodness, no!" said Morgana. "Emily is my assistant."

"Your assistant?" Cerys said. This time she spoke more gently. "Very posh!"

Morgana said to Emily: "We have bloggers coming along for the first time this year. I'm afraid it has caused a bit of an upset. Do you know what a blogger is?"

"Is it someone who writes an online journal or review site?"

"Reviews!" said Cerys, angry again. She threw down her blood-and horseradish-streaked napkin as if throwing down a challenge to any blogger who might wish to take her on. "What gives them the right? I've a mind to start a site of my own, reviewing the reviewers. Then we'd see what's what."

"Cerys is hosting 'Don't Ask Me! I'm Only a Woman' this year," said Morgana quickly. She was obviously keen to change the subject. "You should try to sit in for that session, Emily. If you have ever wondered if women writers mind being patronized, marginalized, underestimated, separately shelved in bookshops and generally sneered at, then the heat and passion in that room should give you the information required to answer the question. Cerys is a formidable champion for romance authors."

Cerys looked as though she could be a formidable champion for just about anything, if she put her mind to it. But now that she knew Emily was not a blogger she relaxed her fists. The rings on her fingers looked like jewelry again, rather than offensive weapons. At last, she smiled at Emily. "Well, it's nice to meet you, love. But if there's a murder on the premises today, don't bother looking for the culprit, it'll be me."

"What on earth's the matter, Cerys?" said the man sitting next to her. The angular lines and hollows in his face were so carelessly perfect, they could have been the work of a gifted sculptor. His gleaming red hair was catwalk-beautiful. He was poetic-looking, but there was a wariness about him, as if he would never relax and put aside his experiences, whatever they might be. Emily couldn't resist speculating. Perhaps he was an ex-soldier? He spoke quietly, and he kept his energy to himself: he didn't look the type to get involved in a bar room brawl. But if someone had aimed a blow in his direction, Emily thought he'd strike back speedily and effectively. Not that there was going to be a brawl here, in the protected five-star luxury of the Coram Hotel.

Cerys sat back down, wheezing slightly. She said, "I've been reading the reviews for my latest book, Archie."

"Ah!" said Morgana. "If only we could all stop doing that."

"Plenty of nice ones, of course," said Cerys.

"Course! That's good."

"Couple of nasty ones, too. Anonymous, mind you."

"Ach," said Archie. "That's one of the sorrows of writing historical fiction, eh, Cerys? We cannae get our revenge by killing bloggers on our pages. It'd be anachronistic."

"And we can't kill 'em in real life, more's the pity," said Cerys, grimly. "There should be exemption from prosecution for authors if the reviews cause mental torment. Remind me to write to the Welsh Assembly about it."

"Archie writes historical fiction under the name of Annie Farrow," Morgana said to Emily.

"Aye," said Archie. "I do."

"Are the books set in Scotland?" asked Emily, politely. She imagined Jacobite rebellions, horses, heather.

Archie grinned at her. "Good guess!"

"Yeah?" said Zena, the big black woman sitting next to Archie at the table. She wore her hair in long plaits piled up on her head and bound with a purple silk scarf. Her fingernails were purple, and her lips were slicked with a shimmer of purple lip gloss. "Archie couldn't be any more Scottish unless he was sitting there playing the bagpipes." She winked at Emily to show there was no offense intended.

Morgana said, "I do wonder if you're putting it on sometimes, Archie."

"You could set off the fire alarm at three in the morning if you want to check," said Emily. "No one's ever more themselves than at three o'clock in the morning in a strange bed."

Morgana stared at Emily, and then she began to chuckle. "Ach," said Archie, which was his way of expressing mirth (and also—as Emily was later to learn—dread, displeasure and disappointment). The other members of the committee joined in laughing.

Emily had a slightly offbeat sense of humor that didn't always sit well with employers, so she was relieved that her fire alarm quip was a hit with the romance authors. It was too bad that she wasn't going to be able to work with them permanently—she might finally have found the perfect job for herself.

"Three o'clock in the morning in a strange bed! Yeah, babes!" said Zena. She shook her right hand very fast several times as if she was trying to dry the varnish on her nails, and exclaimed to no one in particular, "We've got an erotic romance writer in the making here!" Emily was intrigued to discover that Zena sometimes spoke as if to enlighten an unseen audience who were fascinated by what they saw of her life, but likely to be confused by it. It was like living in an audio-described episode of a reality TV program.

Zena leaned forward and briefly grasped three fingers of Emily's left hand with the tips of the fingers of her right in a feminine handshake. She said, "She's met the whole gang now!"

"Except Polly," said Morgana. "Where's Polly?"

"Is Polly one of the bloggers?" asked Emily.

"Polly's one of our most successful authors," Morgana explained. "Polly Penham." Yes, even Emily had heard of Polly Penham. The Sunday supplements were full of stories about Polly's financial and critical success, accompanied by photos of her in her book-lined study, looking calm, poised and clever. Morgana said, "She's made enough money to buy a restaurant. Or was it a yacht?"

Zena said, "I heard she bought a swannery."

Cerys said, "I thought it was a cannery. Though maybe you're right about the swans—isn't her husband a vet?"

"I thought he was a dentist," said Morgana.

Cerys said, "I heard she's going to stand as an MP at the next election."

"Did you?" said Morgana. "She's incorrigible. Dear Polly. I wouldn't be surprised if she did. We're lucky to have her."

"I can't wait to meet her," said Emily. The other authors looked offended. Archie let out a very soft "achhh" that lasted longer than usual. Emily wondered, then, if it was really such a good idea to bring all these authors together in one place, considering how competitive they were. Probably it would be OK, just so long as they didn't turn on her. She imagined a blurry photograph of herself, looking shocked but ordinary, below a screaming headline in one of the true-life-tales magazines that are sold at supermarket checkouts: "What Happens When Novelists Attack!!!"

"Polly will find you soon enough," said Morgana to Emily. "She has something she wants to put in the gift bags that we're giving out later."

"Of course she does," said Zena, not altogether approvingly.

"There are essentially two types of romance author," Morgana said to Emily. "What do you think those two types might be?"

"Historical. And...uh..." Emily was a bit thrown by the question. She had thought that romance novels fell into lots of different subcategories. She looked at Morgana in her jaunty beret. Maybe it was something to do with hats? Authors who wore hats and authors who didn't?

Morgana laughed her smoky laugh. "The two types, Emily, are the ones who are grateful for the free gifts that the organizers have spent three months begging from cosmetics companies, chocolatiers and lingerie shops, and the ones who are not grateful."

Archie, Zena and Cerys cheered up a bit at the thought of the ingratitude of all the other authors who would shortly be joining them for the weekend, and they laughed too, and the mood lightened.

The phone rang at the bar. The barman came over. He was dressed as though he was in a Parisian bar, but he had a strong Australian accent. He said, "I have someone on the line who's asking to speak to one of the organizers of the Romance Writers conference." He stood at the table waiting for a response for a longish time, with no one moving or meeting his eye.

"Would you?" said Morgana to Emily, sweetly.

Emily went to the bar and took the call. In the giant mirror facing her she could see that Morgana was skewed round in her chair, watching and listening.

"Hello?" said Emily into the phone. And then, as much for Morgana's benefit as for the caller's, because she wanted to appear very efficient: "You've reached the Romance Writers Conference at the Coram Hotel. How may I help you?"

"Am I speaking with Morgana?"

"No," Emily said, "not Morgana. This is Emily."

Hearing her name, Morgana made an *unlikely to want to speak to anyone* face in the mirror.

Emily said, "I'm not sure where she is at the moment."

The voice on the other end of the line was almost exaggeratedly American. If a voice could wear a large, white rhinestoned pantsuit, this is what it would sound like. "Hey, Emily," the voice said. "I'm one of the prizewinners. I go by the name of Winnie. You guys might know me as Tallulah, from Tallulah's Treasures? I'm awful excited to meet y'all. Can ya tell Morgana I'll be a little late this afternoon?"

"Yes, of course I can," said Emily. "See you later, Winnie."

"That's mighty nice of you, sugar," said the voice. "Buh-bye." Emily went back to the table to tell Morgana that Winnie would be late.

"Oh, crikey. I hope she'll make it in time for tea with Lex," Morgana said. "She say what time she'd be here?"

She had not. Emily did a passably good imitation of Winnie's accent as she attempted to relay the details of the conversation as accurately as possible. "I go by the name of Winnie," Emily drawled.

"Yes! Winnie. Her name's *Winnie*. Ha ha ha," Morgana said, as if to cut Emily off. She was behaving rather strangely. "That's it. I think we get the gist of it! Is she on her way here, now?"

"Winnie?" said Cerys, when Emily had relayed the message. "Winnie..." She was obviously searching her memory for something.

"Not sure if she's ever reviewed one of yours," said Morgana, a little nervously. "But she's very generous, usually. Four or five stars. A great *friend* to romance authors."

"She sounded American," said Emily. "She said she'd be a bit late."

"She is American. She coincided a visit to English relatives so she could attend the conference," said Morgana. "I do hope we won't disappoint; she was very keen to join us here."

"Bloggers make my blood boil, that's the beginning and end of it. Why can't people keep their opinions to themselves?" Cerys said.

"We hardly want them to," said Morgana. "They help us sell books."

But Cerys tutted and tsked, flicking at crumbs on her lap as if she imagined herself to be flicking minuscule bloggers onto the carpet where they would be crushed beneath her feet.

"Now, the reason I set this up," said Morgana, with an eye on Cerys, "was so that these bloggers would come here and say nice things about us and our books. The three women who've been invited here are winners of a short story competition I organized online—so many book bloggers are also aspiring authors, it turns out—and their prize is to meet us and have dinner, and have a meeting first with my agent, Lex Millington, over tea."

"Lex?" said Zena, sharply. "He's still working?"

"We get a little publicity, and they get a little encouragement," persisted Morgana. "And Polly will drop in and give them some tips about how to get published and make as much money as she does. They'll love that."

"Course they will," said Cerys. "No one ever imagines they'll get published and be unsuccessful."

"No, but it's nice to dream, isn't it? Lex will have tea with them and be charming. He'll talk to them about the industry, which means talking about himself, really. He enjoys that—and they'll enjoy it, too."

"You're messing with things you don't understand," said Cerys, as if blogging was witchcraft. She leaned forward and waggled her forefinger accusingly. Her next words were prophetic: "It can't end well." Then she sat back in her seat and folded her arms.

"So Winnie wrote the best story in your competition?" said Emily to Morgana. She had begun to see that one of the ways she could be most helpful in her temporary new job would be to distract the members of the committee, and calm them when they behaved like tetchy infants. Perhaps Morgana's jingly, soft-toy appearance had some kind of practical application after all.

Morgana blushed. "Well, I wouldn't say that. But she has the most popular blog."

"You can't just write books that make readers feel good, these days," said Zena, seeing—before Emily had time to hide it—that she slightly disapproved of the competition being rigged. "You can't just sit at home and *write*. You got to do competitions and giveaways. You gotta reward people for reading your books. It's not enough that they feel good when they read them, they got to feel good *about* reading them. In other words, you got to get 'em to like you."

"One way to do that is to encourage their aspirations," said Morgana.

"Rrrrright!" Zena bared her teeth, as if—despite what she'd just told Emily—she'd sooner bite her readers than encourage their aspirations. Then she put a spoonful of sugar in her tea, stirred it vigorously, and drank a mouthful, as if she had just swallowed some nasty medicine.

"It doesn't matter how much encouragement you give, you can't teach people how to write," said Cerys. "Good writing comes with practice."

"Ach," said Archie, very softly.

Cerys said, "No offense."

Archie rubbed the palms of his hands on his knees, and then crossed his arms and clamped his hands on his biceps as if to keep his hands still, though Emily noticed his fingers scratching at his skin through his jumper; not in the scrabbly, frantic way of someone who is crawling with ants, but gently, the way that someone might scratch under the chin to comfort a dog or a cat. There was something wary and closed off about Archie. But Emily knew that few writers were as extrovert as the irrepressible Morgana, so Archie's demeanor didn't strike Emily as unusual. But watching him sitting there, hugging himself, Emily also saw that there was something boyish and vulnerable in Archie. He caught Emily looking at him and relaxed a bit, and smiled, as if they were two children in a classroom who weren't paying attention to their lessons.

"Archie was on my Write Back Where You Belong creative writing program," Morgana explained to Emily. "It's where we met. But you're right, Cerys. He's the only one of my students, so far as I know, to be making a living from writing. Studying creative writing is not necessarily a route to success as a writer."

Archie said, "No offense taken."

"It's such a competitive business these days," said Morgana. "I'm not sure we should encourage it." She seemed to want someone to contradict her, but no one did. So she continued: "I had been thinking of asking you all to help me choose a winner from among these three. I know we voted online for these three from the short list—"

"Did we?" said Cerys.

"Did we?" said Zena.

"Yes," Morgana said. "But I'm wondering, should we choose one winner overall and make a fuss of whoever wins at the gala dinner tonight? Or make a fuss of all three of them as we've asked them here and they've been kind enough to come."

"'I don't remember a short list," said Archie.

"I've got the three winners here." Morgana took a sheaf of pages from a plastic wallet in her enormous handbag. "First up is Maggie's."

She put her glasses on her nose. The page on the top had a short passage printed on it. "The brief was to submit a very short romantic story, no more than two hundred words long."

"I don't remember that, M, truly I don't," said Cerys.

"Never mind, I'll read it to you:"

She stood by the hob, waiting for the water in the kettle to boil. She could hear the water bubbling and roiling like her emotions; she watched the steam rising, steadily building like the passion inside her. Steele advanced on soft-soled shoes, his muscled arms swinging.

"Nerida," he said. "I want you. I have to have you."

"No!" she cried. "No, Steele, we can't. We mustn't. You know what Father would say."

But he grabbed her and whirled her away from the hob, and he kissed her, his mouth pressing down on hers.

Though his arms still encircled her, she pulled her face away. "I can't give myself to you now, Steele. I just can't."

But his lips found hers again, his tongue opening her mouth like steam unsticking a sealed envelope. As he pressed the powerful length of his body against hers, the kettle whistled on the hob. It seemed to Nerida as though it was mimicking the song of desire that screamed its urgency inside her mind.

She had told him she couldn't give herself to him now. But if not now, soon. She knew it. He knew it, too.

There was a short silence. Morgana took off her glasses and waited for a response.

"We all have to start somewhere," said Cerys.

"Indeed," said Morgana. "Writing doesn't come as easily to some as to others."

"It's quite ambitious," said Archie. "You've to admire her for that."

"You gonna read this out tonight if it's chosen as the winner?" asked Zena, jolted into speaking like a fairly normal person for once.

Morgana looked anxious. "Well, it won't take long. It's under two hundred words."

"If you keep all three as equal winners," said Emily, "perhaps there wouldn't be time to read out all three stories?"

Morgana looked at Emily gratefully. "Oh, indeed! Yes, perhaps we shouldn't set our guests against each other by inviting them here and then naming one of them an overall winner. It's not very nurturing."

"I take it the others are all of a similar standard?" asked Cerys.

Morgana said, "There was one with a likable, ditzy heroine who had a Maine coon cat. And in the other one the heroine dies in the end."

"She dies in the end and this is a *romance writing* contest? For the love of all that's holy, M! Whatever is the world coming to?"

"You must remember. I put them on the RWGB Forum so we could vote."

"I don't." Cerys shook her head, bemusedly, as though she needed to move it from left to right or she might forget it was there.

"Why do so many people want to be a writer?" Zena said. She looked at Emily. "Don't tell me: you've got a book at home, half-started."

"Oh no!" said Emily. "I don't want to be a writer. I mean, I like reading—"

"What's your favorite sort of fiction, Emily?" asked Cerys.

Everyone suddenly turned to look at Emily. There was a sharp-eyed silence. Which would she choose? Historical fiction, like the books written by Archie and Cerys? Sensual romance, like the books written by Zena? Or how about the contemporary romantic comedies that Morgana specialized in?

A small black man approached the group and hovered. He was slight and lithe, like a long-distance runner, neatly (though rather fussily) dressed in a dull brown suit with a mustard-colored waistcoat. It was a little old-fashioned given that he was probably in his late thirties or early forties. He was wearing light brown leather driving gloves, which had the effect of making his hands look slightly too large for his body. Emily hoped that he would interrupt and save her. But he stood there ever so politely, waiting to be noticed. Emily saw that he smacked his left fist into his open right palm a few times, very gently and quietly, with the restlessness of an impatient man who has never really got used to waiting. Everyone ignored him while they waited for Emily's answer.

After a slightly desperate pause, she said, "I only read nonfiction."

"Verrry good answer. Very good." Morgana laughed and shook her head. The others joined in, appreciatively. Morgana said, "It's difficult to get through these conferences without wanting to kill someone, but if you can get through it without anyone wanting to kill you, you can consider yourself a winner. I can see already that you're going to be a winner, Emily, you really are."

"Mizz Blakely?" said the man in the waistcoat.

"Monsieur Loman!" said Morgana, pretending she had only just noticed him.

"I have brought the chocolates for your ladies," said M. Loman. "Violet crèmes. They have been delivered to the kitchen."

"How kind of you. I think they can go straight into the gift bags. The hotel will deliver them to the rooms tonight."

"Shall I get them?" asked Emily.

Morgana looked at her watch. "Would you?" she said. "And then the gift bags are in the basement conference area, under the table outside the Montagu room. They're easy enough to find."

M. Loman nodded politely and turned to leave. But Morgana stood and grasped his hand. "Your chocolates are one of the highlights of our conference," she said. "The authors do so look forward to receiving them. Last year's raspberry crèmes—mmmmm! I closed my eyes as I ate one and felt *immediately* as though I were strolling through a walled garden in Kent in my negligee, stripping raspberries straight from the fruit canes and cramming them into my mouth, only to find that some superior being, some *God* of confectionery had coated them with dark chocolate. The whole experience was so delicious it just made me want to lie down and die with pleasure." She released his hand and smiled.

M. Loman walked out of the bar with Emily. He didn't seem happy. "These writers..." he said. "These women..." He looked as though the image of Morgana strolling through a walled garden in Kent in her negligee was not something he wanted to consider on a Saturday afternoon.

"She's very lyrical, the way she expresses herself," said Emily.

"But why express it only to *me*, in the bar of a hotel in Bloomsbury?" said M. Loman, irritably, punching his fist into the palm of his hand as he said "me," as if to emphasize the injury this caused him. "Why not have every heroine of every novel discuss the merits of my beautiful chocolates? My Trio of Summer Fruits; my Lime and Coconut Caribbean Delights; my Violet Crème Caresses?"

"They've got some bloggers coming this year," said Emily. "Perhaps they'll mention the chocolates?"

"Bloggers!" M. Loman's horrified expression suggested he might be getting them confused with something he considered unrefined, like truckers. Or muggers. Or joggers.

When they reached the dining room, Emily and M. Loman parted company—he to return to his confectionery shop in Knightsbridge, she to fetch the violet crèmes from the kitchen.

Following directions from M. Loman—fingers thick and clumsy in his leather gloves as he pointed the way—Emily walked through the hotel restaurant to where swing doors marked "staff only" led into a suddenly much shabbier and utilitarian corridor, beyond which was the kitchen. She stared in at the *Titanic*-engine-room steam and noise, at the kitchen staff, and the chefs in their anachronistic uniforms, and she was struck again by the artificiality of the place, and felt again as if she had inadvertently traveled back in time. An angry chef in a white jacket and checked trousers came forward, knife in hand. "No public access!" he hissed. "No! No!"

"I'm trying to find some chocolates that were delivered here," said Emily. She looked past him and thought she saw the boxes of violet crèmes on a table near a door at the back of the kitchen.

The chef pointed to a side door at the end of the shabby corridor that would take Emily outside the hotel, the long way round to the door at the back.

"Are you sure?" Emily asked. "Where does that go?"

"Shortcut. British Museum," he said, and laughed nastily.

Behind him, another of the kitchen staff—a pot washer or porter—stared at Emily curiously as he passed. He didn't look friendly. The chef shouted furiously at him in a foreign language Emily recognized: it was Portuguese (she lived near Stockwell, a part of London that claimed the largest Portuguese-speaking population in the UK; it had the custard tart shops to prove it). But then, deeper within the interior of the kitchen, Emily heard other, shouted exchanges in a language she didn't understand or recognize. Emily had heard—or read, perhaps, in the Sunday supplements—about intrepid young people who crashed private parties in fancy hotels by creeping in through the kitchen. She just couldn't imagine wanting to go to any party badly enough to try to make her way through the hostile men in this kitchen, not knowing if the people around her were threatening to kill her or asking each other if the soup needed more salt.

"A man," said Emily, "the man who delivered the chocolates— he said I should come through here."

The chef shook his head, pointed again to the side door and then folded his arms. There was no way Emily would be allowed to walk through the kitchen. How on earth had M. Loman managed it? Perhaps he had put up his two fists in his gloved hands and threatened the chefs until they let him in. Or perhaps he had just walked round the long way, as she was going to have to do.

She opened the side door and stepped over a pair of polished men's shoes that had been left there, neatly lined up side by side. She was now outside in a smelly courtyard area where the rubbish bins and recycling bins were kept. Emily walked past chest-high, color-coded plastic bins containing empty glass bottles, or kitchen waste, or paper and cardboard. There were cigarette ends on the ground near the door, where people had sneaked out here to smoke. In contrast to the spotlessly clean interiors of the public areas of the hotel, you wouldn't consider eating your dinner off the floor out here.

A chain-link metal fence ran along one side of this ugly, unseen part of the hotel premises; leafy climbing plants had been trained up the fence to disguise it from anyone passing by outside. At the end of this area was a low brick wall, and beyond that Emily saw a housing estate that had been built in the 1970s from gray concrete, now streaked with greenish mossy slime. It rose above the hotel like a malignant ogre that had risen from a swamp and was trying to work out how to take its first few steps; an ogre that wanted to get close enough to swat the pinkish, beautiful brick-built hotel out of its way before stamping off to ruin the beauty of everything else in its path.

The function of the low wall was to delineate the boundary between the hotel and the housing estate, rather than to keep people in or out. There was a gate to the side of the courtyard that could be unlocked for deliveries, and to allow the refuse trucks to collect the bins. Since it was easy enough to walk in through the front door of the hotel, and more difficult to get in to the courtyard, Emily amused herself by speculating that the rubbish in the bins had a higher status or was more valued than the guests. But she knew that it only seemed that way because most of the security in the public areas was more discreet. Subtlety was not important at the back gate.

She thought that security must be an odd business in a hotel because the management *wanted* people to come in and spend money in the restaurant and bar. Visitors were free to come and go. It wasn't a hospital or a prison or a school. But the hotel management wouldn't want members of the public just wandering in and unwrapping a packet of sandwiches and soaking up the atmosphere; it wasn't a public park. Despite attempts to recreate the ambience of a rich person's country house, with Wi-Fi and decent plumbing, a hotel wasn't a rich person's country house and guests were not really guests so much as customers. Security in a hotel like the Coram was bound up with snobbery. It involved letting the right sort of person come in. The people who lived on the estate next door—though it would never be put quite like that—were not the right sort.

Emily was just thinking that no one would ever come this way unless they had to—and it certainly wasn't a shortcut to the British Museum, that had been the chef's little joke—when she saw a pale, graceful woman walking toward her. She had a face Emily recognized but couldn't at first place. Had they met? The other woman was a few years older, around thirty. Was it someone she had seen on TV? Then she knew who it was. There had been several newspaper articles recently about her wealth and success, no doubt timed to coincide with her new book release: it was Polly Penham. "Polly!" Emily shouted, strangely relieved not to be alone here; it was a bit creepy. "It's Emily. From the conference? Were you looking for me?"

Polly stared back at Emily in frank bewilderment for a few seconds. She looked like a fox that has been caught rootling among household rubbish and doesn't know whether to run into the road and risk getting killed by the traffic, or stay put and keep digging until it finds something to eat. "No," said Polly. "I wasn't looking for you. I came out here for a cigarette." She opened her right hand to reveal the long stub of a barely smoked cigarette. It was white tipped, probably menthol. Emily was impressed that Polly hadn't just thrown it on the ground—all the other smokers were much less scrupulous. "Don't tell anyone," Polly said. "I'm supposed to have given up. Did you see that article in *Women's Health* magazine?"

Emily had not. She didn't read *Women's Health* magazine.

Polly shrugged and smiled, a little guilty. "I was paid quite a big fee. I made a fuss about giving up smoking and how wonderful I feel…Is that awful? It was true at the time, but I keep relapsing. Thank goodness my livelihood comes mostly from fiction. Let's get away from this hideous, stinking place."

"I have to get some chocolates from the kitchen," said Emily, pointing in the direction she had been heading.

"Oh, nonsense! You can get one of the porters to do that for you. Or, look, let's ask the manager."

Considering how unpleasant it was out here, it was certainly getting crowded. But here was Nik Kovacevic, walking slowly toward them from the kitchen end of the courtyard, head down, swinging arms covered hand to elbow in grubby gauntlet gloves. His gait was strange. He was wearing galoshes, and he had a cabbage leaf stuck to the sole of his left boot, but it wasn't that. He exaggerated each step, as if he was trying to remember how to put one foot in front of the other. Emily wondered if he had a drink problem. He had almost reached them before he even noticed them. His face was greenishly pale, his lips pressed together as if there was a bitter taste in his mouth.

"Ladies," said Nik when he eventually noticed them. "This is no place for guests. Are you lost? Please follow me." He began to make small but vigorous circular motions with his right arm: a small boy churning up his bathwater to make bubbles. They walked with him back toward the door that would take them into the shabby corridor, and then into the hotel dining room.

"I don't know," said Emily, feeling guilty now for neglecting her duty just so she could get away from the smell of the bins. "The chocolates? They're in the kitchen. I really ought to—"

"They will be delivered to the conference area," said Nik, removing his gloves and galoshes, and slipping his feet into the polished black shoes that had been left by the door. "Allow me to arrange it."

Emily hesitated. She had promised Morgana, after all. But Nik put his arm up to bar her way. He said, "I insist."

"I'll get my books and help you with the gift bags," Polly said. Emily left her waiting in the lobby for the elevator that would take her up to her room, its teasingly slow progress toward the ground floor tracked by the lights on an art deco brass panel. It seemed to hint that guests might have been waiting for the elevator to arrive since the 1930s.

"Don't you wish you had a private elevator that could whiz you up and down really quickly between floors?"

Polly laughed. "Is that all you want? If there's ever a vacancy, I'll be your fairy godmother, Emily."

Emily walked downstairs to the basement conference area where uniformed staff were setting up for the private dinner in the Montagu room later that night, the waiters and waitresses whispering and discreet as they brought in cutlery and glasses on a rattling trolley, the porters shouting instructions noisily to each other as they set up the tables. She looked in and smiled and waved hello. They nodded, smiled or ignored her.

"Yes, miss?" said one of the waitresses, clearly half expecting some daft instruction to break it all down and set it up differently. Her name badge said she was called Maria.

"No, it's fine. Just having a look," said Emily. "Thanks, Maria."

The conference area was a place of low ceilings with no natural light. There was a cloth-covered table on one side of the room, and under it there was a row of gilt-colored paper gift bags with gold ribbons for handles. A big, brown cardboard box had been set on the table. It was stamped all over with branding for Zhush!, a company that made sexy lingerie—presumably its contents were also intended for the gift bags. Emily went up to it and tried lifting it. Whatever was inside weighed next to nothing. Either it was filled with the emperor's new clothes, or something expensively wispy. Emily had lived long enough to know this: the smaller the lingerie, the more expensive it is. So it was probably something wispy.

Polly arrived promptly in a service elevator with a porter, he carrying the chocolates, she carrying a stack of her new paperbacks, *She Knew Too Much*, which were also to go into the bags. Stickers on the front of each copy of Polly's book proclaimed that it had already been chosen for discussion by a television book club.

Emily wondered if any of the other authors ever got jealous of Polly's success. But Polly was too young, too practical, too unshowy, too unpretentious, too helpful to inspire jealousy. Not many people would have stood there and helped Emily pack bags when they weren't being paid to do it. Not many people would have come down in the scruffy service elevator with a porter, carrying her own books. Emily had helped out at enough events like this to know that people's status as a conference delegate was usually too important to them to compromise it by being seen to help with the admin or carry anything that belonged to them.

"Emily!" There was a silvery, jangling sound, and Morgana appeared. She looked anxious. "Darling, any sign of Winnie? Lex is here, and we want to get the tea party underway."

Emily shook her head. "She must be in London by now."

"I'll go and look," said Morgana, with the vague good intentions of someone oblivious to the fact that London was too vast an area to cover with a search party of one.

"Winnie?" said Polly, after Morgana had left. She frowned. "Most of the time I have no idea what Morgana's talking about. I hope Winnie is the name for one of her hats."

Emily laughed. "Winnie's one of the bloggers. She uses the name Tallulah."

"Oh, I see! Tallulah's Treasures? Yes, she's one of our special guests. Should we be worried that she hasn't turned up?"

"I hope not."

But Emily must have looked worried because Polly said, "Do you have any contacts in the police?"

Emily thought of Constable Rory James, whom she had met when she'd helped out at her neighbor Victoria's stage school recently. He had given her his phone number and suggested they meet one night for some Thai food in Brixton Village, which was an engagingly quirky network of covered alleyways with stalls, shops and restaurants in Brixton town center, and not a village at all. He'd had a pleasant manner and soccer player's hips, so she'd said yes. But she had never got round to meeting Rory James for dinner, and anyway he was hardly influential. Not in the way that Polly would mean it. If Polly was going to be an MP and she owned a swannery, she was probably related to a chief superintendent at least. Emily shook her head.

"I have a relative in the police force. Flying Squad but he'll be able to pull a few strings with Missing Persons. I'll give him a call if this woman doesn't turn up by nightfall—put Morgana's mind at rest."

"Is it true you're thinking of going into politics?" Emily didn't want to seem impertinent, but it wasn't something she'd consider doing in a million years, and she'd never before met anyone who'd been tempted by the power/sacrifice trade-off. "Aren't you worried the newspapers will try to dig up some scandal—or find something in your past and make it *seem* scandalous?"

"I've thought about that, and talked it over with Pete—my husband. The kids are too young to consult, so I'll just have to trust that I'm doing the right thing for them. And I'll try and keep them away from the press while they're growing up. I've done stupid things. I used to get drunk when I was younger. I liked to go clubbing. But so what if some reporter digs up a ten-year-old photo of me staggering out of a gay club at five o'clock in the morning? I'm not going to deny anything or hide anything. It's crazy to pretend that other young people—voters—don't do what I did and grow out of it. Making mistakes is a healthy part of growing up. What about you, Emily? Are your wild days behind you?"

"Well…" Emily suddenly felt awfully dull. She always had to get up for work in the mornings, and she valued her precious weekends too much to waste them on headaches and hangovers. "I'm not one for clubbing. I have a little garden I'm really proud of. I grow most of my flowers and a lot of my vegetables from seed. I work in it most evenings if I can. It's really peaceful. Just me and the squirrels and the birds."

Polly laughed. "You're adorable. If you ever go into politics, I'll vote for you, Emily."

"Can I help you girls?" It was Cerys, lipstick on, coat on, carrying her handbag. She didn't look as though she'd come to help.

"We're nearly done, thanks," said Emily.

Cerys took a box of chocolates out of one of the gift bags, and squinted at the label on it. "Violent what?"

Emily laughed, realizing now that Cerys's forceful personality and no-nonsense manner concealed the heart of a clown. Cerys rewarded Emily with a wink. She put on a pair of reading glasses and looked again at the label. "*Violet* crèmes. I see…Very nice…I was just passing. I'm on my way out to the shops."

The basement conference area wasn't somewhere anyone "just passed." Guests had to come down in the elevator or walk down a short flight of stairs to reach it. It had been specially designed, with its own toilets and a lobby area where tea and coffee could be served, so that conference delegates wouldn't intrude on the calm of the main business of the hotel.

"Fair play, I wasn't really passing," Cerys admitted. "I thought I'd come and have a nose."

Cerys was now opening the Zhush! box and fingering its contents, which looked to be frilly and pink. "Remember that year, Polly, when Morgana tried to find a gift that was suitable for Archie?"

"Oh yes!" said Polly. Then, to Emily: "The triple-pack of Beckhamish underpants in medium size that he found lurking in his gift bag made him feel so uncomfortable—not literally, of course, so far as I know, he never put them on—" (Cerys laughed gaily at this) "that in subsequent years she just let him have whatever we're having."

"You don't try and assign a particular gift bag to a particular person?" asked Emily.

"No point," said Cerys. "Too many opportunities to give offense. Imagine if I got a pair of extra-large knickers in my gift bag. I would *not* be impressed, knowing someone—some little twig of a person like M—had determined that extra-large was my size. Never mind that it is my size. We all get the same, and if it's not suitable, we can always pass it on."

Cerys turned over the frilly, rose-colored satin item in her hand, pulling thoughtfully at the black lace edging, and then twanging the black elastic fastening, to test how much give there was in it. Then she held it up against various parts of herself, trying to work out what it was. "I'll be passing this one on," she said, a little disappointed. "It's not in my size."

"Cerys, it's a frilly sleep-mask, not a very small bra," said Polly, giggling. She put one on to demonstrate. She took another out of the box and threw it to Emily so she could do the same. Emily looped the black elastic over the back of her head and pulled the eye mask down over her eyes, leaving a little cheat's peephole at the bottom, like a sly child preparing to play blindman's buff. Emily and Polly stood facing each other across the table for a few moments, peeping out at each other from beneath the padded pink satin of their gigantic black ringed pink eyes, like giggling bush babies.

"Ah, love you! Course it is," said Cerys, good-humoredly. "I won't chance trying it, mind. I've that much spray on my hair at the back, it's turned into a helmet. I could probably come off a motorbike with not a single hair out of place. Still, I don't want to risk mucking it up before dinner tonight."

Serious now, Polly pushed the sleep mask to the top of her head, like a welder in a car repair shop taking a break. She said, "I wonder if Morgana's made a mistake inviting only three bloggers along to the gala dinner."

"Only three!" said Cerys. "What? You want more?"

"There are more than three book bloggers in the world. Think about it—those who haven't been invited are bound to feel left out. It's the bad fairy at the christening syndrome, isn't it?"

"That's all we need. A posse of disgruntled book bloggers stalking the place." Cerys looked around wildly, as if such lawless individuals might already be on their way to attack her. But then all she said was, "Is there a ladies' toilet on this level, do you know?"

Emily pointed, and Cerys headed that way with a wave.

When all the gift bags were packed—it didn't take long—Polly said to Emily, "I'm going for a massage, and then I'll join you upstairs when Lex has gone. I don't want to sit there and listen to him pontificate. You think these gift bags will be OK? No one's going to pinch them, are they?"

Emily thought it unlikely, but she didn't want to offend Polly (the bags contained a copy of her new book, after all) so she tried to look concerned yet noncommittal. Perhaps she just looked vacant because Polly said, "Tell you what, I'll drop by the concierge desk and ask if they can be distributed as soon as possible. I have to pick up a towel for the spa, anyway."

Emily went to look for Morgana. She found her with Lex and two women in the drawing room by the fire, drinking tea. A selection of cakes and sandwiches were displayed on two three-tiered china stands, each layer decorated in a different rosebud pattern; each layer offering bite-size teatime treats (cucumber sandwiches with their crusts cut off, triangles of sugary almond pastries, calorie-packed cubes of chocolaty cake). It looked delicious, and Emily was very hungry. Unfortunately, it would have been bad form to reach out and help herself from the selection—no one else was eating anything.

Lex was leaning back in his comfortable wing-backed chair, talking rather grandly. He was a large white man in his sixties (probably just past retirement age, though of course literary agents never retire: they go on and on, until one day they drop dead of a heart attack when a publisher offers an insultingly low advance on royalties for a favorite client). Lex held a teacup in one hand and sipped from it occasionally when he needed thinking time, or when he wanted to create a slight pause for dramatic effect. He looked like a prosperous legal adviser—which, in effect, was what he was.

Morgana was perched on the edge of a high-backed dining chair, which placed her a little higher than everyone else, like a dignitary at a ceremonial event. Two other women were also there, side by side on a chaise longue positioned close to the fire, leaning forward to listen to Lex. They were Teena Durani and Maggie Tambling, the two remaining prizewinning bloggers. Teena was a slim Indian woman in her late thirties with a sour face and chin-length, dark, shiny hair. Maggie was a white woman in her early forties, plump and pinkish with scraggy brown, shoulder-length hair, her damp fingers with their bitten nails clutching at her handbag as though she feared it might get stolen. When Morgana saw Emily approaching, she got up and left the tea party, and steered Emily toward a pair of high-backed chairs across the room.

"Ugh," said Morgana. "Something dreadful has happened. Just dreadful."

Emily had no idea what she was talking about. Morgana was so dramatic. Emily had seen that the dainty treats they'd been served were untouched. Was there something wrong with the food?

"A woman—a tourist—has been murdered in the estate next door to the hotel. Nik Kovacevic told me it was a drug deal gone wrong. But that's ludicrous, isn't it? To think, the poor woman came all this way…"

"Did you *know* her?"

"Nothing official yet." Morgana put her hand to her face and pinched her nose with finger and thumb. Presumably it was a strategy to stop herself from crying, but her eyes filled with tears anyway. "Oh, Emily. I'm so ashamed of myself."

Emily had a sudden, horrible insight. "You don't think it's Winnie?"

"American people are so trusting. So innocent. I should have met her at the station. I should never have set this thing up. I only invited her because I thought it might benefit our gathering this weekend—I put our needs before hers." In her distress, Morgana began to speak in phrases that sounded like the titles of romance novels: "*I Put Her in Harm's Way. She Has Paid Too High a Price. An Innocent Creature, Exploited!*"

She set Emily off on a riff on crime titles: "*Blame Solves Nothing. Too Late to Help Her Now. No One Knew She Would Die.*"

There was no telling how long the two of them might have carried on like this. Fortunately, they were interrupted by the sound of raised voices from the party by the fire.

"I don't consider myself a romance writer," Teena was saying. "Mostly, I write upmarket fiction."

Emily wondered at the crassness of someone who would turn up at a romance writers' convention and speak scornfully about the work they produced. (And what was "upmarket fiction" anyway?) She looked over to see what Lex would make of it. He had a discomforted expression, as though he was suffering the aftereffects of a gassy lunch, and trying not to break wind. "My dear Teena," he said, calmly but a little too loudly. "In the publishing industry, we don't usually—"

But Teena interrupted him. "I thought you were going to take us on as clients." She sounded aggrieved, and vaguely threatening. "I wonder what my readers would say about all of this."

"Well," said Lex. "I hardly—"

"We can get *advice* in the magazines. We can go to an online forum if we want"—here Teena put her fingers into the air at either side of her face and made rabbits ears with forefingers and middle fingers, to denote quotation marks—"a 'chat about publishing.' This is my *time* you're wasting here. I'm never going to get it back."

Emily reflected that Teena would not get back the time she had spent chatting with Lex, even if she had spent it doing something she considered more worthwhile (like chatting to the Queen of England, or inventing a cure for cancer), because that's the way time works. Surely that was obvious? But Maggie, the other blogger, was now hunched over with both arms around her handbag, as if she thought Lex might dip into it to steal her money as readily as he had stolen Teena's time.

Emily took a large notebook out of her handbag and began to write up the notes from the recent committee meeting:

NOTES FROM THE RWGB COMMITTEE MEETING:
Though none of the committee members remembered voting for the three shortlisted winners, two of the three winners are here. The third, unfortunately, has gone missing. The winners are all bloggers, chosen with the hope that they will write favorably about the conference. It remains to be seen whether this plan will be a success.

But as she wrote, she started to get distracted by some of the discrepancies in the information that had emerged, and she began to think about those instead.

It was odd that no one remembered voting for those pieces of writing, as if the poll had been rigged. But who rigged the poll? Morgana?

Polly wandered up to Emily's table with Cerys and Zena, and Emily shut the notebook. Polly raised her eyebrows in an amused inquiry.

"Poetry," said Emily. No one ever asked to look at another person's poetry.

Polly's hair was still damp from the spa. Cerys and Zena were wearing their outdoor coats. Emily noted that Cerys wasn't carrying shopping bags, and anyway hadn't had long enough to visit the shops and get back to the hotel since she'd last seen her. What had Cerys been doing since visiting Emily and Polly in the basement?

The romance authors stood around Emily's table with their backs to Lex and the bloggers so they wouldn't get drawn into the discussion. But they listened very carefully.

"Teena seems rather put out," said Polly in a low voice.

Morgana hurried back over to join them. "It does seem a little *odd* to denigrate romance writers, when we're hosting this event." She also spoke in a low voice. She had a face that might have turned Teena to stone, had Teena gazed on it.

Cerys stood with her arms folded and nodded. She pursed her lips and made an *I'm saying nothing* face.

Polly said, "You don't think she'd try to expose Lex, do you? On her blog?"

"Goodness no!" Morgana said, "None of those accusations were ever proved!"

"Look, I know you believe that criminals can be rehabilitated—" said Zena.

"Lex is not a criminal," said Morgana.

"You're not streetwise, Morgana," Zena continued. "Where I come from—"

"I hate innuendo, Zena. Innocent until proven guilty. It's a law that applies in North London just the same as anywhere else."

Polly spoke calmly, reasonably: "Teena just wants a leg up in the business, doesn't she?"

"Everyone wants a leg up," said Cerys. "Youngsters these days! What's wrong with doing it the hard way like the rest of us? Learning your craft." She put her arm through Zena's. "Come on, love. I've earned it, I'm going to spend it. Let's get out there quick, or we'll no sooner arrive at the shops than we'll have to turn round and come back."

Emily wondered why Cerys hadn't gone to the shops half an hour ago if she was so keen.

Zena wasn't quite ready to go yet. "Poll, babes. Where'd you get that cardigan? I'm looking for something like it in purple."

Polly blushed and shrugged her narrow shoulders. Her little pink cardigan scarcely looked big enough to be used as a bonnet by Zena, who was big boned and meaty, and incredibly buxom. "Oh, this old thing?" she said. "I don't remember."

Cerys was used to catching her grandsons by the scruff of her neck. She reached out and grabbed the collar of Polly's cardigan, and turned the label out for all to see. "Topshop. I can't even find a pair of tights to fit me in there. Good luck getting a cardigan in your size, Zeen."

Cerys and Zena left to go shopping, arm in arm.

"Don't be late for the dinner, will you, darlings?" Morgana called after them.

Polly neatened the collar of her cardigan. "Any news on the missing blogger?"

From just behind Polly, Morgana made frantic *no* signs with her eyes.

"Uh, no," said Emily.

"Well, if you want me to do anything…" Polly said.

"This is the most stressful conference I can ever remember," said Morgana, huskily. "I'm gasping for a cigarette. You're lucky you've given up, Polly."

Polly winked at Emily, half-guilty, half-conspiratorial. "I miss it sometimes," she said.

There came the sound of Teena's raised voice again. Morgana said, "No cigarette breaks for the wicked. I have to go and sort out that little lot." She hurried over to where Lex, Teena and Maggie were sitting.

"Poor Morgana," said Emily. "'With great power comes great responsibility.' Was it Voltaire who said that?"

"My son insists it's Spider-Man. Either way, you know it's got to have been a man. Women don't have to wait to become powerful; we deal with responsibility every day—everything from worrying about birth control to doing the weekly shop."

"Men do the aphorisms; women do the dishes," Emily suggested.

Polly laughed. "I hope one of us can find a way to keep you on after the conference, if you'll have us. If it wouldn't be too dull?"

"I don't know anything about writing." Emily couldn't see herself taking dictation under the circumstances in which romance novelists are generally believed to create their work, with a lap full of dogs, in an office heavily perfumed and decorated somewhat tastelessly in shades of pink.

"Oh, it isn't just the writing. I've got kids…a restaurant, various business and political interests. I'm based in Buckinghamshire, that's the only catch. Nice and quiet for the kids. Great for writing. But maybe a bit quiet for someone your age?"

Was Polly Penham offering her a job? It was tempting. Emily couldn't imagine leaving her home in South London to go and live in Buckinghamshire, busying herself with timetables for Polly's children's piano and karate lessons. But Polly's interest in Emily seemed genuine. Emily gave Polly a big, warm smile. How did she manage to take an interest in other people, write full-time, have children, and a restaurant, and a swannery or a cannery or whatever it was?

"You're amazing."

Polly responded by giving her a quick hug. "Emily, you really are the sweetest thing."

As Polly headed back to her room, for Emily's benefit—she knew Emily was watching—she walked exaggeratedly softly past where Morgana sat with Teena and Maggie, so as not to attract their attention, like a cartoon mouse.

"Polly! There you are." Morgana was too canny to be outwitted by someone pretending to be a cartoon mouse. "Do come and join us, and give Teena and Maggie some tips about how to imitate your success."

Emily smiled at that. But she soon turned serious again and opened her notebook and tried to get her thoughts in order. Could Winnie really have been murdered? If so, by whom? Random strangers? Muggers? Angry bloggers? One of the members of the RWGB organizing committee who had brought her here? What had Lex been accused of in the past? Was his lack of appetite a sign of guilt? And what had Cerys been doing, in between telling them in the basement that she was going shopping, and finally leaving with Zena just now?

Emily made a few notes about the things that were bothering her. Rather than try and make sense of it now, she thought she would write down everything as it came to her and ponder it later. She wrote:

Lex, Cerys, Nik Kovacevic
Cigarette butts
Chefs, kitchen, bins

Hairspray!

Who killed Winnie, and why?

What absurd, suspicious thoughts! She was light-headed from lack of food, and it was making her fanciful. Lex was not likely to have murdered anyone. Cerys had probably spent at least twenty minutes putting hairspray on her hair, doing plenty of damage to the environment but not actually *killing* anyone. Anyway, she wasn't even sure that Winnie was dead. Wasn't it more likely that the woman who had been found on the estate was not Winnie at all, and Winnie had just gone shopping?

Emily looked over at Polly and the two prizewinners, and eavesdropped as shamelessly as the organizing committee had done. Polly had an easy way with people that Emily admired. As she sat with them by the fire in the drawing room of the Coram Hotel, Teena and Maggie gazed at Polly with something like love.

Polly looked the way you might want your mummy to look if you were nine years old and the product of a chaotic and slatternly home: she was neat and clean and calm, and her outfit was the color of strawberry ice cream. But that wasn't why Teena and Maggie admired her. They admired Polly because she wrote best-selling books.

"I hope this won't be too dull for you," Polly was saying. "What do you talk about at bloggers' conferences?"

"We don't have them. Not really," said Maggie.

"What *would* you talk about?"

Maggie and Teena were silent. Maggie looked alarmed, Teena resentful, as if they suspected this was some kind of test.

Polly was unperturbed by their failure of imagination. "You'd probably talk shop, wouldn't you? Why the five star rating isn't enough. Something like that."

"Yes!" Maggie had cheered up a bit. "Yeah, there's some books I'd like to give six stars. Or ten stars, if I could. Like yours...Polly."

She used Polly's name hesitantly—a school-leaver meeting a teacher in the pub and being invited to discard the usual honorific.

"Or zero stars," Teena said.

Teena could probably find something sour to say if she watched an orphan opening a present on Christmas Day. If Emily had been responsible for rigging the poll to choose who should attend, she'd have done her best to keep Teena away.

But Polly's response was upbeat. "Teena, that's what I love about book bloggers. First of all the frankness. And also the inventiveness. Why get stuck with a five star system if we don't like it? Why not six stars or no stars?"

"How do you write, Polly?" asked Maggie. "What is it you do that makes you so successful?"

There was really no answer to this. Polly sat down and wrote, and then she revised what she wrote, and then she revised it again until she was happy with it. And because she was really good at it, what she ended up with was acceptable to Polly, her editor, her publisher, her readers and the reviewers. But that wasn't the answer Maggie and Teena were looking for. They wanted a secret shortcut.

Polly bought herself a few seconds of thinking time by passing the plate of French Fancy cakes with colorful fondant icing and grittily sweet cream inside. Teena and Maggie both took one, as though being offered a cake by Polly might be the first step on the road to publication.

For those who were desperate for success in a creative field, Emily could see that it would be difficult to try and imitate the "manufacturing process" because it takes place inside a person's head. So it would be tempting to believe that mimicry of your hero or heroine's mannerisms, or the faithful recreation of their working environment, might enhance the chances of success. For some, the mimicry would involve boozing. For others it would be shopping.

Or smoking. Or fishing. Others would wish for a bare room to write in, or a room full of books. For others it might mean moving to London or Paris or New York, or having a house by the sea. Perhaps it wasn't the method of imitation that mattered, but the ritual—the acknowledgment that one needed to create space in one's life for the muse. If so, then perhaps Teena and Maggie hoped the act of picking up a bright yellow cake (Teena) and a bright pink one (Maggie) from a china plate proffered by Polly would stimulate the flow of brilliant writing.

"I could tell you what I do. But each of us is different. Let's talk about *your* writing, shall we?" Polly clasped her hands together for a moment, as if praying to the gods of creativity.

Consciously or unconsciously, Teena clasped her hands together, too. "I'm all right once I get going. But its intimidating sitting there, looking at a blank page."

"Let's talk about how to kick-start our writing engines. Have you heard of automatic writing? Morgana swears by it. And she's the master when it comes to masterclasses. Notebooks ready, ladies? Pens?"

From their expressions, Teena and Maggie might have been suicide bombers at Heathrow Airport, asked to remove their jackets. Polly sensed their anxiety and moved to reassure them.

"I won't look at what you've written! This is just a warm-up. Let's think about a big event in our lives, but write about it from the point of view of someone else involved in it. Instead of trying to create something from nothing, we'll be like forensic investigators, uncovering the truth about what happened, and why. Yes? After that we'll talk about what it *feels* to write; how we feel as writers. Sound good? We can share our thoughts and learn from each other. That's what we're here for."

Emily could see that Polly had indeed hit upon the best way to deal with Teena and Maggie, which was to flatter and involve them, and encourage them to talk about themselves. Who, after all, wants to listen to someone like Lex impart knowledge? Very few adults make good students, and Teena and Maggie were not among them. They had come here longing to be taken seriously as writers. They were about to get a taste of what they wanted, as Polly gave their voices equal credence with hers.

Poor Winnie, Emily thought again. Missing all this. She closed her notebook and picked up a snack menu from the table in front of her and studied it. She hadn't eaten any breakfast and she was hungry. She needed to eat in order to think. Unfortunately, almost everything on the menu had meat in it—vividly described meat: succulent pork from a speckled Somerset pig; tender beef from a Highland cow; moist breast of chicken from a woodland-dwelling, free-range fowl; etc. Emily was vegetarian. Perhaps she could have a plate of chips. She looked at the menu and was unsurprised to see that these were not just any old chips. They were thick farmhouse wedges of fluffy Maris Piper potatoes, twice-fried and served with sour cream and piquant—

"Hello!" a man's voice interrupted her. "I'll buy you something to eat if you're hungry."

She looked up and blushed bright red. It was Constable Rory James, dressed like an ordinary member of the public. Surely he hadn't come all this way just to...?

"I'm investigating a murder," he said, cheerfully. "*Detective* James now. Do you mind coming along with me?"

CHAPTER THREE
GIANT CAT

The facts, as Detective James ("Call me Rory") explained them, were these: The body of an American woman tourist had been found in the estate next door to the Coram Hotel, propped up next to the wall that separated the housing estate from the hotel. She had remained there for a while because she had looked peaceful; any local resident who had noticed her had assumed she was drunk, and sleeping off the effects of alcohol. Street drinkers were not uncommon in the area, though (unlike most of them) the woman had been dressed smartly, she was alone, and she was not accompanied by a friendly dog on a leash made out of a piece of string. Eventually some youths had approached the woman and determined that she was dead, at which point the police were called.

Their inquiries established that the woman had checked into the Coram Hotel earlier that day, for a total of two nights. The cost of her first night's accommodation had been met by the Romance Writers of Great Britain. The woman's name was Winnie Kraster. She lived in Connecticut and, prior to arriving in London, she had been visiting relatives in Milton Keynes. An officer had gone up to Milton Keynes to interview the relatives. Winnie's husband had been informed of her death and was on his way to Heathrow.

"You're helping to organize the Romance Writers' conference, aren't you? Do you remember meeting Winnie at all?"

"I didn't meet her. I spoke to her on the phone." Emily recounted the details of the conversation she'd had with Winnie as accurately as possible.

Det. James didn't say anything for a short while. He seemed to have something to say that was going to be a bit awkward, and he was trying to find the best way to express it. Eventually he said, "It's human nature to want to see ourselves at the heart of a drama."

Emily wasn't sure where he was going with this. The last time they'd met, she'd helped to save the lives of some children in an end-of-term show at a theater school. There had been plenty of drama then, not all of it onstage. But she didn't think Det. James wanted to chat about old times. She remained quiet, waiting for elucidation.

They were in a small, pretty meeting room on the ground floor of the hotel. It was called the Virginia Woolf room—presumably for no other reason than that the hotel was situated in Bloomsbury; there was no evidence that Virginia Woolf had ever visited—and it had been commandeered as an interview room by Det. James. It had an inlaid marble fireplace and was furnished with two art deco lamps. Emily was impressed to see that the jug of iced drinking water that had been supplied by the hotel had slices of both lemon and orange floating in it, and there was a plate of pastries and cakes on the highly polished wooden table where Det. James leaned to write his notes. Though he had offered to buy her something to eat, Emily didn't want to order it and then sit there and wait for it, and then eat it in front of him, so she had refused the offer. Now he saw her looking at the plate and pushed it toward her. She chose a Florentine and a macaroon and ate them greedily, licking her fingers when the chocolate from the Florentine melted on them.

Det. James said, "Winnie was from Connecticut. She was born and raised there. I've already spoken to her husband. People in Connecticut don't speak like that, Emily. You're doing an accent from somewhere…I don't know…the deep south. Mississippi or some-where. You sound like Elvis."

"That's how she spoke," said Emily. She blushed bright red. She resented the idea that Det. James—Rory—thought she was making a drama out of it: enjoying this poor woman's death.

He said, "There's something else that doesn't quite make sense."

"You said she checked in this morning, but she called after that to say she'd be late."

"Yes."

"It is odd," admitted Emily. "But I'm telling the truth. Maybe she didn't want us to know she was here, so she could do some shopping?"

"Yes." Det. James looked embarrassed. "But think about it. If you want to change your mind about anything you've told me, let me know."

"But you haven't told me the most important thing," Emily said. "How did she die?"

"It's rather strange, actually. Her neck was broken. We think that's what killed her. But she had other broken bones, and cuts and bruises on her body."

"What was it? A violent mugging?"

"It seems nothing was taken. Her handbag was found with the body. It was like…like…have you ever seen a cat playing with a mouse? It was like a giant cat picked her up and played with her and killed her, and then set her down quite gently. The body was posed by the wall like she was asleep."

Emily shuddered.

"Keep all this to yourself for now."

"Her death, you mean?"

"Not that. It's been on the news. The Chief Super's been ap-pealing for witnesses. Doesn't look good, does it? An American tourist walks the streets in broad daylight and she's attacked. No, I mean keep the details to yourself."

"Had she been moved very far, do you think?"

Det. James closed his notebook and smiled. "You're asking a lot of questions, Emily."

"She was a guest at the conference. I'd like to help, if I can."

"OK. You think of anything else you remember, bring it to us."

"Poor Winnie."

Det. James stood and walked with her to the door of the room. He held it open for her, politely. "These things are really rare, so don't go worrying, OK?"

His words were meant to reassure, but they didn't.

When Rory had closed the door behind her, Emily took her notebook from her bag, leaned against the doorjamb and wrote *Giant Cat*. Then she went to look for Morgana.

CHAPTER FOUR
COCKTAILS

Morgana was in the bar, drinking a cocktail, a pile of shopping bags at her feet. Nice life! But as soon as she spotted Emily, before Emily could say anything, Morgana jumped down from the bar stool, grabbed Emily's hands and gibbered, "Blogathon! There's a blogathon!" Morgana seemed to be genuinely frightened. Emily looked around the bar, but she couldn't see anything. What on earth was a blogathon, anyway? It sounded like a made-up creature. A dragon in a kids' story, something like that? *And then the blogathon roared and all the flowers in the garden shuddered and closed their petals in fear...*

Morgana got back on her bar stool. She motioned for Emily to sit. She whispered, "It's a kind of online event."

"Oh! Bloggers? That kind of blogathon." She was starting to sound like Cerys.

"In commemoration of Winnie. It's taken off like wildfire. It's like Princess Diana all over again." Morgana drained her glass.

"It's not your fault she's dead."

"I'll be doing some sort of tribute in my welcome speech tonight, of course. But I rather think that's not soon enough. We need to handle this now. It might...Nik said..." She stopped, and shook her head. It was too much.

"Nik said what?" Emily was prepared to hate him for whatever he had said.

"Nik said they've started ringing up. Members of the public who've seen it on the news. They want to come here. They want to hold a…" She couldn't say it.

Emily tried to guess: an inquest, a party, a banner, a puppy, a picture of Winnie, a…

"A vigil," said Morgana. "Zena's gone to see about it—if we can get a room for them to meet in. They're going to mass here, and those who can't get here in person will join the blogathon online. She thinks we ought to have a press conference before it gets out of hand. There's anger out there. Here was this woman, this innocent, blameless woman, and we lured her here, and she died, alone and friendless."

"Well," said Emily, awkwardly, "you're not going to say that at the press conference, are you?"

The barman set down another cocktail—it was orangey colored, with black bits in it. Passion fruit? Now didn't seem the time to ask. Morgana rallied a bit. She said, "No, darling. Of course not." She knocked back half her drink.

"Cocktails are so delicious, aren't they? I always find it difficult to tell how much booze is in them."

"You're a sweet girl, and very tactful. Don't worry, there's hardly any booze in these at all. I have to face the press, and I need a little boost from the sugar syrup in here. I shall be quite sober."

Cerys came rushing in: "I've heard the news from that young policeman. Anyone else been interviewed?"

"Yes," said Morgana.

"Yes," said Emily.

"That poor woman! Her poor family. Breaks my heart to think of her beaten to death by a pack of animals, dying there all alone. We gonna cancel, M? We can't carry on, it's disrespectful."

"How can we cancel? Check-in's at three. People are starting to arrive. I'm calling a press conference. We can use it to express our sincere regrets for the loss of this woman's life, and draw attention both to the role of romance writers in spinning dreams that distract from reality, and the way that we can address social issues and important matters of life and death in our pages."

Zena approached, stately as a queen and trimmed with purple silk: both Cleopatra and her barge.

"Who've we got coming, Zena?"

Zena picked up the shopping bags Morgana had been guarding for her—Emily was amused to see a Topshop bag with something pink inside it among them—and sank into a comfy chair. To answer, she had to look up at Morgana, perched on her stool by the bar.

"I got my man Trevor coming along."

"Oh, good! *Daily Mail*?"

"*Ham & High*," said Zena.

"Ham and High?" Cerys said pleasantly, picking up the menu from the bar. "That sounds delicious." She winked at Emily to include her in the joke. "I think I'll have one of those."

"The *Ham & High* is a local newspaper, not a…a toasted sandwich," said Morgana. She giggled.

The other women laughed companionably, and Emily finally saw the friendship between them, as they tried to defuse the tension of the day with silliness.

"Ladies?" The Australian barman interrupted the laughter. He held up a phone attached by a long wire to the extension in the bar. "Call for an Emily Castles."

The call was from Polly, speaking in the kind of groany, ultra-weak voice people normally reserved for calling in sick to work.

"Emily? I need help. Can you come to my room?"

"Polly?" Emily was so obviously alarmed that the others looked round, concerned. "Polly?"

But the line was dead.

CHAPTER FIVE
POISON

Emily didn't wait for the elevator. She ran up the stairs up to Polly's room on the second floor, ran along the corridor and knocked, and waited. What if Polly was unconscious or...?

Polly wasn't unconscious or dead. But she was obviously unwell. She opened the door for Emily and then lay on the bed looking paler than ever, with bluish lips and sweat on her upper lip. She had been sick—there was the sharp, unmistakable smell of it coming from the bathroom.

"I think there's something wrong with the chocolates," Polly said. "I took a bite of one and..." She shuddered and lay back on the bed, eyes closed. A small trickle of drool appeared at the corner of her mouth, which she wiped with her fingers. "I've called a doctor."

Emily handed her a tissue. "Maybe we should get it tested for, I don't know, can you get salmonella in chocolates? We should get it tested to see if there was something wrong with it."

"Good idea," said Polly. "But I flushed that one." She lay quietly for a few moments, and then she said, "There was a weird taste in it. Rancid, like...peanuts that have gone off. Or...no, not peanuts. More like...almonds. But horrible and bitter."

"They had something nutty inside? Praline? You're allergic to nuts?"

"No, I'm fine with nuts." A slight note of exasperation. "The one I bit into had purple fondant inside, like you'd expect. There weren't any nuts in it. But it didn't taste right. I spat it out. You think it could have been tampered with?"

"Who'd want to do something like that?"

"We left the bags downstairs for a while after we'd put the gifts in them. Someone could have come along and tampered with the chocolates."

"I can check with the staff—see if they saw anyone hanging about down there. But it's more likely to be food poisoning, isn't it? Or stress, maybe? Worrying about Winnie."

Polly seemed irritated by Emily's determination to find a reasonable explanation. Emily was interested to see this side of the normally calm Polly. Obviously she was one of those people who get a bit needy when they're ill.

"What if I saw something or heard something or said something that makes me a target for the same person who killed Winnie?"

This wasn't needy. This was narcissistic. Emily felt embarrassed for Polly. And then she remembered how Detective Rory James had felt sorry for her earlier, when he hadn't believed her story about the phone call from Winnie, and she tried to be less judgmental. What if there was something wrong with the chocolates? She considered the practicalities. There were around forty conference attendees who were currently checking into their hotel rooms. How many of them might be tempted to start on the chocolates before dinner? Probably quite a few. Unless they could be sure that something else had made Polly sick, she'd have to make arrangements to get the violet crèmes removed from the gift bags before anyone else ate them, as a precaution.

Emily let the doctor in when she arrived. She was a calm-looking woman in her fifties with watery eyes and thread veins at the sides of her nose. She plonked her medical bag on the dressing table. While

Polly described her symptoms, Emily withdrew slightly and looked around Polly's room for clues to her condition. Was there anything here that could have made her ill? There was a nearly full pack of white-tipped menthol cigarettes on Polly's dressing table. Well, those were no good for her for a start. Just by the pack of cigarettes there were around a dozen bottles of various shapes and sizes containing astringents, exfoliants, eye cream, face cream, hand cream, body lotion, nail varnish, nail varnish remover and various other potions and lotions that Emily couldn't distinguish from the labels at a distance.

"Perhaps there was something you spilled on the chocolate and accidentally ingested?" She was rather proud of using the word ingested, hoping to impress both Polly and the doctor. "Nail varnish remover's poisonous, isn't it? Something like that?"

Ignoring her, the doctor said rather irritably to Polly: "There's no reason to suspect poisoning. An upset tummy is a more likely explanation. You want to watch out for dehydration. Make sure you drink plenty of water in the next few hours, and take it easy. We *could* do a stool sample. But you seem to be recovering."

The threat of a stool sample seemed to be for Emily's benefit, to make her unpopular with Polly.

Emily went to the dressing table and picked up a bottle at random, squinting at the label for the name of an ingredient that sounded poisonous. This particular preparation claimed to combat "the seven signs of aging." And those were what, exactly? Emily tried to come up with a list: thinking the country's going to the dogs, going to bed early, visiting National Trust properties—

Polly called over in her sick-day voice, "I didn't drink any nail varnish remover, accidentally or deliberately."

The doctor said, "Vital signs are normal. Temperature is normal. You have a slightly elevated heart rate. Have you had a panic attack before?"

"No," said Polly. "I'm not sure I'm having one now." She tried to look insouciant, but she was so pale, and she hardly lifted her head from the pillow, so she just looked tired.

The doctor went into the en suite bathroom and washed her hands thoroughly. Emily followed her. The doctor said, "You know, it's dangerous to give an antidote to poison if poisoning hasn't been confirmed. Do you understand? You're risking the patient's life." She dried her hands and left.

"You want me to stay for a bit?" Emily hoped that Polly would understand this question was a formality, like asking the host at a party if there's anything you can do when you arrive—you don't actually expect to have to chop onions or vacuum the carpets or bath the children. Similarly, Emily didn't want to stay by Polly's bedside, she wanted to get away from the vomity smell in the room and get back to helping Morgana.

"You're a sweetie. Thanks for coming to see if I was OK. I didn't say thank you, did I?" Polly's charm was returning, together with a healthier complexion. "I'm all right. You go ahead. I'm going to sleep it off. I'll be down later if I feel all right. And Emily?"

"Yes?"

"Take care of yourself. If someone tried to hurt me because of something I saw or heard…Well, we were both prowling around where we didn't belong, weren't we, at about the time Winnie was killed?"

"When we saw Nik Kovacevic?"

"Everyone's saying no one saw Winnie when she checked in, and that's not quite true, is it?"

"Who did she see?"

"The staff at the hotel, of course. And whereas normally a tourist would be on their guard against strangers in a foreign city, they'd trust the staff, wouldn't they?"

"You don't think Nic Kovacevic killed Winnie?"

"No. I don't know what I think. Just be careful, that's all. I know you want to find out what happened to Winnie and you're worried about me. But don't go snooping about in any dark places. And don't eat the chocolates!"

Emily went back to her room to get her chocolates. She had no intention of eating them. She planned to give them to Det. James for testing. She put them in her handbag, then she went to find Morgana to tell her about Polly. She found her in the bar with Cerys and Archie.

"Ach," said Archie. "Have y'ever met an author who didn't think they were dying of at least one rare disease? Imagination plus Internet equals hypochondria."

"She'd definitely been sick, though."

Morgana caught the barman's eye and signaled for another fortifying drink. "She might have picked up a bug in the Jacuzzi?"

"Love, you can't take any chances," said Cerys. "Besides, it's a verruca you'd get in a Jacuzzi, not cyanide poisoning."

"Cyanide!" exclaimed Emily. She hadn't mentioned cyanide…

"Hold your horses. It's not a confession. I may write romance, but I read my share of mysteries. That taste of bitter almonds you described—that's cyanide."

"Aye," said Archie. "It is."

"Darlings, Polly is a very imaginative person, and of course we love her for it. But while I don't doubt she thought she could taste bitter almonds in her chocolate, I doubt *very much* that she's been the victim of cyanide poisoning. Why can't she stick to self-diagnosed lupus, suspected RSI and a headache-that-might-be-a-brain-tumor, like the rest of us? Still, we can't take any chances. Emily, I'm going to go along with your suggestion that the chocolates be removed from the gift bags as a precaution, though the delegates aren't going to be happy if all they get in this year's gift bag is a frilly sleep mask and one of Polly's books."

"I could look in the gift shop?"

So Emily went to Ye Olde English Gift Shoppe on the ground floor of the hotel. There she bought forty cellophane-wrapped packets of vanilla fudge. The purchase was funded by Morgana, and it cost her ninety pounds. Morgana also thought it wise to tip the hotel staff another twenty pounds for their trouble. As she forked over the cash, she said, "You see why no one else ever volunteers for the position of chair of the committee, Emily?"

So Emily headed to Nik's office with forty packets of fudge to ask him to find someone from housekeeping to substitute them for the violet crèmes in all the rooms belonging to the RWGB conference delegates. On her way there she saw one of the waitresses who had been setting up the dining room in the basement conference area earlier.

"Maria! Did you see anyone suspicious hanging around by the gift bags after we'd filled them earlier on this afternoon?" Emily was careful not to couch the question as though it was an accusation—when anything goes missing in a hotel, everyone always blames the staff. She didn't want it to look as though she was really saying, *Did you take anything from the table?* She added, quickly, "Nothing's missing, it's not that. I'm not accusing anyone. I hope you don't think that. I just wondered—did you see anyone?"

Maria said, "No."

"Did you see Nik? The manager?"

"No. No one."

"I was there, and Polly Penham. Do you know her? Pink cardigan?"

"Yes."

"And Cerys—with the blonde hair? And Morgana popped down for a bit, too—the one with the hat? But did you notice anyone come along after we left?"

"No. No one came."

"Thank you." Emily gave Maria her loveliest dimpled smile and went into Nik Kovacevic's office.

Nik was busy at his computer, typing a review for the neighboring Fitzrovia Hotel on a popular travel review site:

```
     After reading other reviews for the
Fitzrovia, my husband and I were looking
forward to staying in what we had assumed
would be a very classy hotel. It was
our wedding anniversary and we wanted a
special weekend away to celebrate. Imagine
our dissapointment when our room was not
ready when we tried to check in. Things
went from bad to worse when we finally went
up to our room. The decor was tired and
the plumbing less than satisfactory. When
we called down to Reception to make our
feelings known, the staff were unhelpful.
We will not be recommending this hotel to
our friends. Do not make the same mistake
as us. Save your money!
```

Prompted to give a rating and a suitable heading for his review, he wrote: 1★ Dissapointing.

He had noticed that people who complained about goods and services online were often "dissapointed," the sibilance of the extra *s* endowing the word with a resentful hiss. Therefore he too misspelled disappointment and disappointing for the sake of authenticity. Women wrote more reviews than men, so he also had got into the habit of writing reviews from a woman's point of view. He had no strong wish to trash other hotels. He really didn't. But he suspected that the practice of writing phony reviews was widespread, and he felt he had no alternative but to reciprocate. The service and facilities at the Coram were impeccable, as he knew at first hand. Yet every week or so there would be another critical review with a one-star or two-star rating on one of these travel sites. How was he to make sense of it, except to assume that rival hotel staff were leaving these absurd complaints? And how was he to counter these practices except to write a few of his own?

The desk was side-on to the door to Nik's office, and Emily had approached quietly and quickly. Before he'd had time to close the window on his computer, she had got close enough to him to read what he was writing and get the gist of the review. Nosy cow! But if she had seen what he'd written, she didn't let on. She had an armful of vanilla fudge and a head full of crazy notions, so perhaps she hadn't looked at his computer.

He listened to what Emily had to say. When she was finished, Nik was briefly offended on behalf of everyone, everywhere who had ever had to have dealings with the general public.

"Tainted? I don't think Cyril Loman would send you tainted chocolates. There must be some mistake." Nevertheless, at her request he called for housekeeping to take care of it. He stood and extended one arm toward the door to show Emily out.

Emily had chosen the word tainted over poisoned because she had thought it would cause less offense. She hadn't started well, but then she'd hardly started at all. There was plenty more she wanted to say to Nik.

"The woman who died—"

"The one who died *on the estate*? Very unfortunate. Nothing to do with the hotel, of course." One arm extended again, politely.

"I wondered if she could have fallen from her room."

"No. Her bones would have been shattered, wouldn't they? I heard she was sitting propped against the wall."

"Yes, I know. But she'd been posed like that. Her neck was broken."

"A violent sneeze, perhaps?"

"A sneeze?"

"There was someone I was at school with who broke his neck playing rugby. Thing is, he didn't realize it; he walked around like that for years. The doctors found the fracture years later in an X-ray. Said that he was a walking time bomb. He could have been paralyzed just by a violent sneeze." Nik became quite animated, remembering the story. Emily didn't doubt that it was true. She just didn't think it relevant.

"I was thinking, you see. Could she have been having a crafty cigarette and fallen out of the window?"

"None of our windows open wide enough for a toddler to slip through, let alone a grown woman. We take the safety of our guests very seriously—and we're wise to the wiles of smokers. No. She was killed by thugs next door on that estate."

"I just...the idea of her being killed by thugs is so horrible. So violent."

"I wouldn't walk through that estate myself late at night. Couple of the kitchen porters live there, and they walk together for protection. Tough blokes, too—from war-torn countries. Who'd think it, eh? Living through a civil war in Africa and then scared of walking alone in Bloomsbury. It's the young kids with knives—no respect for human life. They don't understand consequences. You see it all the time on the news."

Emily didn't believe that the porters were frightened of walking through the estate. "The policeman I talked to said it looked as though she'd been picked up and dropped by a giant cat."

"That's their theory is it? A giant cat's responsible for that woman's death?"

Nik wanted to be getting on with his day. He stood and picked up a file at random from his desk, trying to signal that he had finished talking and that he had work to be getting on with, without being too rude.

"No, it was...an expression. A way of explaining something inexplicable." Emily frowned. Nik wasn't being very cooperative. "But it made me think she might have fallen."

"Be that as it may, this poor lady died elsewhere. There's no need to drag her body back over the threshold, so to speak. Let's leave this business outside where it belongs. We work hard to create an atmosphere of calm, here. It's not just me—there's a whole network of people, mostly unseen, who rely on the hotel for their livelihood, and strive to keep it going to the best of their ability. People who have never worked in a hotel find it difficult to appreciate, but we function like a family. And it's not just the workers that I have to think about, of course. Our guests need to feel that they're cosseted and protected once inside our walls. I don't want to disturb them by suggesting a stronger link between the hotel and this poor lady's murder than the fact that she was planning to stay here. I'm sure you understand."

Emily did understand. Nik didn't want Winnie's death connected to the Coram.

"Is there CCTV in the hotel?"

Nik looked startled, and then irritated, and then he recovered himself. Emily was really getting under his skin. She was forcing him to look at her, really look at her and try and work out why she was bothering him so much, while reappraising his own sense of himself. It was like a romantic comedy, without the romance or the comedy. He saw an earnest, inquisitive brunette with a dimpled smile. And he knew that she saw an evasive, slightly sweaty man with a narrow, angry face and a cheap suit. He put his left hand up and smoothed a lick of his hair with his palm. He said, "We'd consider it an invasion of our guests' privacy to have CCTV inside the hotel."

"Outside, though? You must have it outside."

"We do have security cameras outside. Yes."

Now they were getting somewhere!

"But the system was undergoing a reboot earlier today."

"It had been turned off!"

"The system was being reset."

"So there are no pictures around the time that Winnie was killed?"

"That's correct. Though of course it would show nothing anyway, since she was *killed on the estate.*" Nik smiled and touched Emily's shoulder very lightly. He couldn't give her a shove, much as he would like to, so instead, like an angry poltergeist, he used the sheer force of his will to propel her the three paces to his office door. She really would have to leave, whether she considered him rude or not.

Outside Nik Kovacevic's office, Emily paused to write a few quick notes: *reboot, back over the threshold.* She'd managed to get a look at Nik's computer before he'd closed the screen. This prompted her to write: *one-star reviews.*

Emily was heading back through the lobby to the Virginia Woolf room with her trio of chocolates to give to Det. James when she heard a voice calling her name.

A middle-aged woman with short gray hair, wearing a timeless (or, to put it another way, unfashionable) dark-green corduroy jacket and skirt and a maroon paisley shirt, stood at the check-in desk and waved her silver-topped cane cheerfully. "Emily!" she called. "Yoo-hoo! Emily!"

It was Dr. Muriel, Emily's neighbor. Emily offered to carry her suitcase up to her room so that they could talk about Winnie's death. Dr. Muriel was an academic who was used to sifting information. She could help Emily sift the information she had gathered so far.

By the time they had waited for the elevator, got the key card to open the door and gone into the room, Emily had just about finished explaining what she had learned. She put the suitcase on the floor and went to try and open the windows. None of them moved more than an inch at the top of their frames. Dr. Muriel neither protested nor expressed approval of Emily's apparent fanaticism for fresh air. She sat on on the red velvet chaise longue by the window and put her feet up.

Emily handed over her notebook apologetically. "It's just a jumble at the moment. I thought I'd write down everything and then worry later on about what's relevant and what isn't."

"Good idea. Very interesting," said Dr. Muriel as she scanned the pages.

"Yes, but as you can see, I wrote down some of those things just because they irritated me. They're about me, not Winnie. But then there were other things that were niggling at me and…I don't know. I wrote down anything that didn't make sense in case it might have some bearing on what happened to Winnie. I'm still sorting it all out in my mind."

"Now, if you were an undergraduate I'd suggest using sticky labels and different categories for your notes. Undergraduates like sticky labels."

"So do I. I can't get excited about bags or shoes. But I really love stationery."

"So you see, looking at this, you'd have categories like...*Emily, Winnie, hotel staff, smoking, litter...*"

"I really hate litter."

"Me too."

"I think that whatever I was investigating, or whatever notes I was writing, I'd end up having a category for litter. Trouble is, just because someone drops litter, it doesn't necessarily make them a murderer."

"Indeed not. But perhaps the custodial sentence should be about the same. It would make a marvelous deterrent, eh?" Dr. Muriel gave a rather vulgar laugh, as if someone had just told her a dirty joke. "What troubles me most is this business with Polly."

"You think she's in danger?"

"Do you?" Dr. Muriel liked asking questions. She didn't much like answering them.

"She could have been targeted because of something she has seen or heard," said Emily. "But I'm not sure what."

"It's anomalous. A woman dies. Another may have been poisoned. The poisoning doesn't fit, does it? It's too elaborate. As if a page from one story has got mixed up with another." She handed back the notebook to Emily. Emily opened it up and wrote *anomalous* next to the other words, as much because she liked the sound of it as anything else: *I'll have the anomalous, please, with a spoonful of blueberry flummery and a pot of tea.*

"I'd say we need to stir things up, don't you, to find out what's going on?" Dr. Muriel picked up her cane and made poking motions before using it to heave herself up from the chaise longue.

Emily didn't think that was wise at all and wondered whether she should say so. She didn't actually know Dr. Muriel very well, except to say hello to in the street. While it was true that they had briefly been imprisoned together in a cellar in a very large house in Brixton during a fireworks party, they hadn't spent the time exploring each other's foibles and eccentricities. It had seemed more important to look for a means of escape. But Emily was starting to see that her outwardly staid neighbor was a maverick. If she was set on stirring things up, Emily doubted that there was any point trying to dissuade her. She followed Dr. Muriel to the elevator with a sense of foreboding.

The elevator bell dinged as it reached their floor. The polished doors opened and an elderly couple got out. Dr. Muriel and Emily got into the elevator, joined at the last minute—Emily had to hit the "doors open" button to accommodate him—by a short, skinny Mediterranean-looking kid of about thirteen.

"Ground floor?" Emily asked sweetly as she let go of the "doors open" button. He ignored her and pressed the button for floor number five. "Oh," she said, as the elevator began its steady ascent. "We were going down."

Dr. Muriel treated Emily and the boy to her vulgar laugh. At the top of the panel there was a button labeled "Roof Terrace and Bar." Dr. Muriel saw it and nodded toward it for Emily's benefit, "Our giant cat?"

"You may be right." Since they were going that way anyway, Emily pressed the button, but it wouldn't light up.

"That floor's closed," said the boy. He hitched his trousers up and smirked. "You can't go up there till six o'clock." He looked smug, the way boys of his age do, until hormones suddenly add twelve inches to their height and they discover rebellion, girls, music and inscrutability.

Emily pressed the button for floor number six, and when they reached it they got out and looked for a staircase to take them up to the roof terrace on the next level. They found a staircase marked "Emergency," and up they went. The door to the rooftop bar wasn't locked, and they went inside. The nighttime glamour of the place was lost without uplighters, candles, music, the murmur of guests and other mood enhancers, though the picture windows on three sides gave a good 270-degree view of the landmarks of the surrounding area of London. To the north, a wall blocked out the less-delightful view of the tower blocks of the neighboring estate.

Emily and Dr. Muriel walked through to the open-air terrace that adjoined the bar. It was a very pleasant area with a dab of bright green lawn, some evergreen shrubs in heavy, blue-glazed clay pots, and a stone fountain that was not currently operational. There were mint-green parasols sunk into cement in mint-green pots, to anchor them in high winds. The parasols were closed for now. Everything up here was closed or turned off. But it was still pretty.

They took a look around. There was a hip-high metal and reinforced glass fence around the edge of the terrace. Weighted pots containing plants and decorative shrubs had been placed in front of the fence, to screen out the sound of the traffic below, or the wind, or both, and presumably to discourage guests from getting too close to the edge.

If Winnie had fallen, she surely had fallen from somewhere else on the roof terrace. Behind the aubergine-colored leaves of a Japanese maple tree in a blue pot, next to the bar, Emily saw a little wooden door. She pushed it open and found herself in a small, ugly service area with bins. The fence here was a low metal one. Directly below was the courtyard that led to the hotel kitchen.

Emily looked over the fence to get a better look. Her foot kicked at a loose, moss-covered stone which skittered and clattered to the ground below, making Emily sway slightly as she watched it fall down toward the colored bins in the courtyard below.

"Careful!" said Dr. Muriel.

Emily retreated from the fence. "Let's say Winnie's being chased by someone; she's frightened and she's trying to get away. She darts in here, thinking she might be able to hide. She looks down and sees those big plastic bins full of bottles and cardboard boxes and whatever. The attacker follows. She decides to jump, hoping the boxes will break her fall."

"But she lands awkwardly and breaks her neck?"

"I suppose so." Emily looked down and saw the trees in Russell Square across the street, and then, when she went up on tiptoes, leaned forward and looked to the left, there was the entrance to the hotel running the length of the building. Ornate black railings demarcated the hotel's property. These enclosed narrow, designated strips of pavement where guests could stand and smoke without mixing with the hoi polloi on the street beyond. There were a few smokers out there now.

To the other side of where the smokers were standing was the courtyard with the plastic bins, screened from the hotel entrance by a wall. Emily walked to the far end of the rooftop bar's service area and looked down. Below her was a scrubby playing field, a scruffy children's playground with a roundabout and a slide, and the low wall that separated the estate from the hotel.

Dr. Muriel followed. "And why was Winnie up here?"

They went to the low railings and stood there, looking down. Emily felt a little bit dizzy. She took one step back. "I don't know," she admitted. "Maybe she wasn't being chased. What if she was meeting someone? Someone she trusted."

"It wouldn't take much to unbalance someone and give them a shove. But you'd need to temporarily distract or disable them. A sudden, warlike scream would be very effective. But not practical, in case someone heard it…You'd need something—some *thing*…"

"Like chloroform?"

"Pepper spray, perhaps."

"Hairspray?"

"That would do it. But who would arrange to meet in this horrible bit by the bins up here?"

A look down at the litter at their feet answered that question. Smokers.

"Winnie didn't know anyone here. She checked in early, but none of us saw her."

"Someone saw her," said Dr. Muriel, grimly. "But why would the attacker risk moving her, when he or she might so easily have been seen?"

"It's like the killer's trying to say something: to make some point."

"Indeed. But what?"

CHAPTER SIX
THE PROTEST

Emily went along to the Virginia Woolf room with her trio of chocolates and handed them over to Det. Rory James. She said, "I'm having all the chocolates from the rooms brought down to you so you can test them for poisoning."

Rory was filling out a form. He put his pen down and pushed his chair back a couple of inches from the table, and he looked up at Emily. He didn't say thank you. He said, "There's a lot of paperwork involved in something like that." He said it in the tone of voice of someone who doesn't relish paperwork.

Emily spoke quickly, hoping that her enthusiasm might transfer itself to him. "If the poisoned chocolate was meant for Polly, then the only time it could have been tampered with would be *after* it had been put into the gift bag, or after it had been put into her room. If all the chocolates are poisoned, then it could have been done at M. Loman's factory or in the hotel kitchen. But then whoever was responsible would have ended up a mass murderer if we'd all eaten them. That's not very likely. It means that Polly was probably the target. But we need to know, don't we? So do you think you could get them tested?"

"I can see that you're anxious about this. Your friend's ill. Someone has been killed in the vicinity of the hotel." He smiled. He looked tired. He was in his shirtsleeves. Emily could feel the heat coming off him—not sexual heat. Just long-day-at-work, tired heat. Emily wondered how soon it would be before Rory became a hard-bitten maverick with a disastrous private life, like the police detectives she saw on TV. She felt very sympathetic toward him. But then he said, "Look, if I could prove to you that this isn't poisoned, would it make you feel better?"

He snatched up the packet of chocolates, opened it, removed a violet crème, sniffed it, broke it in two pieces. He put the smaller of the two pieces in his mouth. His eyes held Emily's as the chocolate-coated purple fondant melted on his tongue. The air between them was tense, and there was a challenge in the way he looked at her, as if he was accepting a dare and wanted her to admire him for it. She did admire him for it. It was audacious, an act of bravery that summed up his fury about all the endless paperwork that was now part of his job. She thought, suddenly, how beautiful it would be if all protests against bureaucracy—if all protests against everything—could involve warm, tired men in clean shirts silently gathering to put chocolates with mauve-colored centers in their mouths, and melt them on their tongues while holding the gaze of young women standing across from them, with humor in their eyes and bravado in the set of their shoulders. More entertaining than student protests, anyway, which—whatever the wrongs and rights of it—were always a bit scruffy and shouty.

But as well as being admirable, there was a little part of Rory's chocolate challenge that was somehow also patronizing, as though he needed to demonstrate to Emily that she was worrying unnecessarily and creating drama where there should be none.

"It's actually very nice," he said after a few moments. "I don't think it's poisoned." He didn't reach out and eat the rest of it, as Emily might have been tempted to do—perhaps he didn't want to cross the line between using an unorthodox method to test the evidence, and consuming the evidence because it was delicious. Maybe there were even rules about not eating luxury handmade chocolates on duty, just as there were rules about not drinking on duty. He shrugged and grinned, inviting Emily to relax and forget about it.

"At least we know we're not dealing with a mass murderer," said Emily.

"Makes my job a bit easier!"

"Will you make a note, though, that she was sick—and about the taste of bitter almonds in the chocolate she ate?"

"I will." He didn't pick up his pen and write anything. "Anything else? Any other theories?" He smiled engagingly, a naughty, happy light in his eyes. He must get precious little opportunity to be cheerful at work. Still, Emily wasn't going to indulge him in this. She maintained a lemon expression. But she couldn't stay quiet for long because she had another question.

"Would you need two people to move a dead body?"

"Not necessarily. It depends on the strength of the person doing the moving and the weight of the body."

"But if you had to lift the body over a wall? If you had to do it quickly?"

"Well," Rory sighed—a teacher tiring of a precocious child. "In that case four hands would be better than two, I'd say. Wouldn't you?"

A maid knocked on the door and came in. A badge on her breast advertised her name as Lydia. She was a chubby Filipina woman of about thirty, wearing a pale lilac uniform dress and sensible shoes. She had a careworn face. She could have been a nurse on duty, except that she was carrying a gift shop bag full of violet crèmes.

"What I do with these?" Lydia asked.

Rory didn't look at Emily as he said, "Thank you, uh…Lydia? Perhaps you could dispose of them for us?"

As Lydia left with the chocolates, Emily slipped her the twenty pounds she'd had from Morgana.

Rory said, "You must leave this to us, Emily. There are procedures to be followed. It's not just me working on this investigation, you know. We haven't even had the pathologist's report yet. I can't tell you everything, but we know what we're doing."

Emily left the room, closed the door and got out her notebook. Then it occurred to her that she ought to write down the exact time that Rory had eaten the chocolate, just in case it contained a slow-working poison and he was found, cold and dead and slumped over the paperwork he hated.

With that horrible image in her head, she burst back into the Virginia Woolf room, with the passion and breathlessness of a romantic hero who can't pass up the opportunity to say "I love you!" to the heroine, and chases after her and…

Rory looked up at her, half-smiling in spite of himself, like a toddler reacting to a game of peekaboo.

"I just wanted to check you were OK. You know, the chocolate…"

He grinned. He was OK.

Emily withdrew, shut the door, and left him to it.

CHAPTER SEVEN
THE VIGIL

So Emily was now looking for two people working together—one of them possibly armed with hairspray, at least one of them a smoker—who had pushed Winnie off the roof terrace or contrived to make her fall, and then heaved her body over the wall into the neighboring housing estate for reasons unknown. She glanced around the public areas of the hotel, and *everywhere* there seemed to be guests sitting in pairs, or members of staff working in pairs. But how many of them were capable of murder?

When she got to the bar she saw Morgana and Dr. Muriel sitting together talking over their notes. Dr. Muriel poured black coffee from a pot on the table into a cup in front of Morgana. A silvery jingle of bracelets and a hiccup accompanied Morgana's cheerful wave. As Emily approached, Morgana said to her friend, "Thank you for recommending Emily. She's been *such* a help."

Emily was conscious that she'd hardly done a stroke of work. Sometimes, she'd noticed, people liked you more, the less work you did. If you came along and tried to do things your way, or did everything too quickly and showed everyone else up, then you could make yourself unpopular. Sit on your arse all day, or chase about following up clues to a murder, and people were unstinting in their praise.

Another silvery jingle called them to attention. "Darlings, I need to make a plan for this evening."

"I thought you'd put me next to that old rogue, Lex Millington."

"Not a seating plan, Muriel. A *plan* plan. In fact, the committee's meeting shortly to make a plan, but I need a plan for that meeting. We're in a terrible pickle. A poor woman has died, and there's to be a vigil at the hotel. We have a press conference arranged, and I need to find something suitable to say about the whole affair. It's not in my nature, as a novelist, to make things *less* dramatic. I need your help." Morgana hiccuped.

"Ah! You think, as an academic, I can help make everything seem dry and serious?"

The two old friends smiled at each other.

Emily said, "Is there anything you want me to do?"

"We're in for a long night, Emily." Another hiccup. "You take a breather, if you like. You want to meet us back here in fifteen, twenty minutes? We can inspect the arrangements for the vigil before the press conference. I'm not looking forward to being confronted by an angry mob."

"You're worrying unduly, Morgana. You're always too hard on yourself. Even a mob could not fail to be charmed by you." There are people who, having discovered that some people like sticky labels, will offer sticky labels to everyone. Dr. Muriel was not one of these. While she might have discovered that her undergraduates liked sticky labels, she knew only too well that Morgana preferred reassurance. So she was handing that out in dollops, washed down with strong black coffee.

Emily wasn't quite sure where she should go or what she should do with her "breather."

"All right, then. I'll go and…" She faded away without actually saying what she would do.

Inevitably, she started turning over the day's events in her mind. Whatever Polly had seen, she might have seen. Did that mean she was also in danger? As for *who* they had seen, that had been Nik. Emily didn't much like him. But that didn't make him a murderer. Still, she thought she might have another look outside. What had he been doing out there when she and Polly had run into him? He had seemed very keen to shoo them away and back into the hotel.

Emily walked through the dining room—she saw Maria, and nodded at her—and then, when she thought no one was looking, she slipped through the door leading to the kitchen, walked along the shabby corridor, and went out of the white door that led to the courtyard with the bins. What was she looking for? How would she find it? How would she know if she'd found it? She didn't know. This wasn't going to be a methodical approach. She simply hoped that if she kept an open mind and looked around, the information she needed would present itself. Whatever it was, she had to find it fast and get out of there before anyone (before Nik) saw her. Though the area looked much as it did when she was there earlier in the day, it now seemed to have an atmosphere as unpleasant as its smell. It seemed eerie.

There were cigarette ends discarded on the floor, as before. Emily moved quietly, looking at the ground, then looking up at the hotel. There were no guest windows overlooking this area, but she could see the low fence surrounding the service area at the back of the bar on the roof terrace. She tried to visualize the trajectory of a body falling from there into the courtyard below. She saw that it might land in one of the large, colored bins about twenty feet in front of her. Red was for waste food. Yellow was for paper and cardboard. If Winnie had landed in a yellow bin, the contents might have acted as a mattress, stopping Winnie's bones from shattering and her skin from bursting open, and her organs falling out. Emily walked cautiously toward a yellow bin—and stopped, hearing a scrabbling sound from inside the capacious red bin next to it. A rat? A dog? A man? A murderer? She cringed, reflexively making herself smaller. Should she investigate or turn and walk away?

The decision was made for her when her mobile phone rang. Emily was scrupulous about turning her phone off when she was in the theater or the cinema. She never answered the phone in the bank or at the counter in the post office, or when paying for purchases in shops. She'd have to add "when investigating the possible scene of a temporary resting place for the body of a murdered woman" to the list—next time. If there was a next time.

Emily pulled her phone from her handbag and hit the red button to cut off the call, while simultaneously swiveling and ducking behind a large, yellow bin behind her. As she went down, the head of a man bobbed up above the lip of the red bin. He looked around. Had he heard the phone? Had he seen her? Was any part of her still poking out from behind the bin? Anyway she could see him. It was M. Loman.

"Hello?" he said. He was dressed in his smart suit. He was not dressed appropriately for going through the bins. "Hello?" he said again. He ducked down inside for a few moments, and then he threw a black, plastic bin bag out over the side. It was filled with something bulky. Next, he put his gloved hands on the lip of the bin and heaved himself out, quite elegantly, as if heaving himself out of a hotel swimming pool. "Henri?"

Emily watched as one of the porters came up to M. Loman from the other direction. They stood close to each other, whispering in French. Henri was small and dark like M. Loman, presumably hailing from the same country of origin. They shook hands once, in a brief, businesslike way. Then M. Loman picked up his bulky black bag and began to walk toward where Emily was hiding.

It was no use. M. Loman would walk right past her and was bound to see her. Emily would have to stand up and make herself known. Seeing a familiar face in unusual surroundings would be rather awkward, like going on holiday to Thailand and seeing a neighbor on the beach. She wondered what the correct greeting should be, under the circumstances. *How nice! What a surprise! Lovely day for grubbing about in the recycling bins—find anything useful?* None seemed quite right, especially as he was carrying a...what *did* he have in that bag?

"Hsst!" called Henri. M. Loman turned, looking slightly disoriented. Henri jerked his head in the direction of the wall that separated the courtyard from the estate next door, and M. Loman walked away from Emily, following Henri toward the wall.

Peeping from behind her yellow bin, Emily saw Henri stop and crouch at the bottom of the wall, making the crook of his arm into a kind of step for M. Loman to use to climb over. M. Loman threw the black bag before him, then followed it over the wall and disappeared. Henri brushed himself down, looked around warily, then went back in the direction of the kitchen.

Emily waited until she was sure he had gone, then she went and peered into the red bin. The interior was pretty revolting. There was a deep layer of discarded foodstuff, and an opened-out cardboard box on top of it with footprints on it—M. Loman had presumably been standing on the cardboard to stop his shoes sinking into the quicksand of rotting detritus. There was nothing inside the bin that seemed linked to Winnie's death—but then, if there had been, and M. Loman was in some way connected to it, she'd hardly expect to see it; he would have been there to remove it. Certainly, he had removed something. But what? Emily had hoped to gather new information out here, but whatever she'd gathered hadn't helped her to solve the mystery of what had happened to Winnie—it had just given her something else to puzzle over.

Emily walked back to the restaurant. She turned her mobile phone back on and checked to see who had called her. It was Morgana. She went to find her in the bar.

Emily walked with Morgana and Dr. Muriel from the bar to the Brunswick room. It was one of the small function rooms on the ground floor that was normally reserved for private dining or day-time seminars. It had been set aside for use for the vigil, and it was being supervised by Zena and a local bookseller, an amiable-looking, youngish man with a ponytail. Zena waved them in, and Emily saw that a book of condolences had been left open on a long table in the middle of the room. On either side of it were two computer screens. One displayed the home page of the Tallulah's Treasures blog, with a winsome picture of Winnie in her prime and, under it, the words RIP. Another had a scrolling display of blogs that had joined the blogathon, posting personal memories of Winnie-as-Tallulah and tributes to her. The reminisces were touching, even though some of those posting had only ever met Winnie online—or perhaps, Emily reflected, that actually made it more poignant, because Winnie's online friends would now never have the opportunity to meet her in person.

Against the far wall, another table carried the latest titles from members of the RWGB, together with a pile of novels labeled "Tallulah's Top Ten Picks," and copies of a book called *Publishing without a Parachute (How I Stopped Worrying and Learned to Fly)* by Lex Millington. Emily picked it up, hoping to find a clue to the accusations against Lex, against which Morgana had so vehemently defended him. But she only saw that the book seemed to be some kind of gossipy insider's guide to the publishing industry, and had been blurbed by Jonathan Franzen as "the most important book about publishing you will ever read" and by Oprah Winfrey as "a classic."

Three woman sat in a semicircle at the other side of the room. They seemed to have gathered for the vigil. When they saw Morgana they looked vaguely hostile. But all three held copies of Polly's latest book, which they had purchased from the ponytailed bookseller. They warmed up a bit when Morgana went over and greeted them, and explained that Polly had been taken ill but would be along later to sign books.

Zena called over from the table, "Not just Polly, babes. We're all prepared to spend as long as it takes signing books, in Tallulah's memory. It's what she would have wanted, yeah? Tallulah loved signed books."

As she talked, Zena held up a copy of her book, *Starlight Falls*. Morgana nodded. The semicircle of three nodded. But none of them took the hint and bought Zena's book. It was a shame, because the pitch had been done smoothly and professionally—Zena would have been an excellent choice as the host of a TV shopping channel, and her nails looked good, which is important when the cameras go in close on a product.

Two more people came into the room—a man and a woman in matching blue anoraks. They looked at the computer screens and read some of the blogathon tributes. The woman signed the book of condolences. She seemed upset. She blew her nose loudly. The man—her husband, perhaps—had the resigned, nothing-to-do-with-me air that men affect when they accompany their wives on shopping trips. The woman looked around. After signing the book of condolences, there wasn't much to do. She wandered up to the bookstall and picked up one or two of the books, turning them over in her hands. Presently she chose both Morgana's new book and Polly's. Her husband paid for them, and Morgana graciously autographed the copy of her book. In purely commercial terms, it looked as though this tragedy might turn out to be something of a success.

Emily got out her pen and looked in her handbag for her notebook. Then she realized she had caught the attention of the others in the room. They watched her standing there pen in hand, and they expected her to write in the book of condolences. She hesitated and then decided to go for it. *Dear Winnie*, she began. What next? She had no fond memories to share. Simply writing RIP sounded a bit...hip-hop. She read a few of the previous entries, hoping to take her cue from them. But she didn't feel comfortable suggesting that Winnie was looking down on them. In fact, it only made her think of Winnie looking down from the roof terrace at the yellow bin below, or falling into it. She looked further back in the book. What had Teena written? *It's a competitive world, Winnie, but you died a winner. RIP, Teena.* That was nice. Some of the others had taken up the Winnie's a Winner theme in their entries. Just copying everyone else didn't sit well with Emily, either. Finally she decided on *I'm sorry I never got the chance to meet you.* And then she remembered her dog, Jessie, dying in her arms at a very old age, not so long ago. She thought of how desperately upset Winnie's husband Des must be, on his way to a foreign country to be with his wife's body, knowing he'd never see her alive again and hadn't been with her when she died. And it set her off. She wiped away a few tears. The woman in the blue anorak handed Emily a tissue, and Emily blew her nose. She felt both hypocritical—as if she was pretending to have known Winnie and to have cared about her more than she did—and slightly relieved and vindicated. What was the point of a vigil without a public display of sorrow? Grief for strangers these days was oddly competitive.

That word again. *Competitive.* She wrote it in her notebook. Maybe she was just echoing Teena's words. Maybe her investigative notes were just a mild form of plagiarism? In that case, she might as well go the whole hog. In her notebook she wrote *Winnie's a*

Winner. And *RIP*. She stuffed it in her bag before anyone could see. The people sitting around here were so poorly served for entertainment that if any one of them should ask what was in the notebook and she should say poetry, they might actually ask her to stand there and read a bit of it aloud.

"Should I stay and help out here?" Emily asked Morgana.

Zena replied for her, "Naw. We're all set, babes. That Teena girl come and set up the computer screens for me. I got Frazer there selling the books. We got the banqueting people bringing in the members of the public who turn up for the vigil, and they've promised to keep 'em out of trouble and feed 'em fancy snacks. Zena's taken care of it. It's all in hand."

"I need you next door, Emily," said Morgana. "I need you to take notes. But I value your input, too. Thank you, Zena. You've been wonderful. We've all pulled together in the aftermath of this tragedy. We've shown what we can achieve under pressure."

"I'll let you into a secret, babes. You want something, you visualize it, yeah?" Zena came close to Morgana and lowered her voice. She smelled of incense and toothpaste.

"Yes. I suppose I do."

"Well that's not enough, M. Not with all the competing wishes and dreams being visualized all around the world by so many needy people. And London's majorly bad with the high density of population: all want, want, want. So what I do, I give my visualization a boost. I create something that represents what I want to happen, and I light some incense, and I say out loud what I want to happen, and I ring a little silver bell to draw attention to my prayer. And then, that brings success. I don't ask much for myself. I'm basically a spiritual person. I hold back from asking for things for myself all the time. But if you want something, do that. It works."

"Oh, I see. That's useful to know."

"Don't go cheap on the incense. Nothing stinks so much as a cheap joss stick."

"No. OK. Thank you. Yes. Where's Teena? I'd like to thank her, too."

"She went to meet Polly. To talk about writing."

"She's not with Polly," said Emily. "Polly's been taken ill."

Morgana stepped aside to allow two more women to come into the room. They were carrying flowers in cellophane. There was something ghoulish about the way they were all gathering, silently, in memory of someone they had never known. They came into the room with the solipsistic entitlement of people who are grieving. They seemed confident that they had a right to be here. But once they had taken their seats they looked around expectantly, as if in anticipation of a pleasant evening. They were not like bereaved relatives or friends; if anything, they reminded Emily of hobbyists meeting for the first time at a convention to celebrate whatever it was they collected or practiced.

"Hobbyists is a *nice* way of putting it," whispered Dr. Muriel loudly, when Emily confided her thoughts. "Zombies—that's what they remind me of. The undead coming to claim their own. There seems to be no way of staving off their approach, except with one of Zena's romance novels." She demonstrated by picking up a copy of *Starlight Falls* and holding it in front of her, as if she was a vampire killer holding a bible. When she took a step forward, boldly, and waved the book around, the grieving vigilers shrank back slightly. Dr. Muriel replaced the book on the table with a wink at Emily.

"I saw something very strange just now," whispered Emily. She told Dr. Muriel about M. Loman with his bulky black bag, going through the bins.

"Do you have your notebook?"

Emily handed it over.

"Yes," said Dr. Muriel, reading and nodding.

"What?"

"Yes. Yes." Dr. Muriel handed back the notebook. "Very interesting."

"I know we thought it must be two people working together. But it can't be Cyril Loman and Henri, surely?"

"I have no idea, m'dear. You'll solve it, I'm sure."

Two more women shuffled forward and placed their flowers on the floor beneath the book of condolences, still in their plastic wrappings. Morgana gave them a tragic smile, which was greeted with mild hostility, and then she signaled discreetly that it was time to leave.

Archie and Cerys were waiting for them in the Captain Thomas Coram room, a wood-paneled meeting room on the first floor. The members of the committee, and Emily and Dr. Muriel, joined them at a large round table in the center of the room, their hands almost touching, as if they were planning to take part in a séance. The mood was somber. Emily took out the pen and notepad from her bag, ready to make notes.

Morgana said, "I need your help to find something to say about Winnie. Now, I know very clearly what I *don't* want to say. I don't want to come out with meaningless phrases like 'not on my watch' or 'her beloved.' Don't you hate it when someone dies and they liked something and it's 'his beloved Arsenal,' 'her beloved cat.' Actually, this woman did have a cat. That much we know, at least. I've got the skeleton for a statement—I've been going over it with Muriel, who has been curbing my flourishes so that when I speak, it doesn't sound like a blurb for a tragic love story. Cat. Husband. Other than that, we just know so little else about her. We know that she died, but not how or why, never mind what sort of person she was. I mean, anyone can love a cat."

"Not me," said Cerys. "They bring me out in blotches, all up my arms."

Archie spoke up: "Have they no further info, then? The police?"

Dr. Muriel, sitting to Emily's left, said, "I wonder…could Winnie have been killed because she was part of the One Star Club?"

The door banged and Polly came in and joined them, ghostly pale, as if the séance had begun, and the words One Star Club had summoned her there.

CHAPTER EIGHT
THE ONE STAR CLUB

"The One Star Club?" Polly said, suspiciously. "I've never heard of it."

"Is it something I ought to mention at the press conference?" asked Morgana.

"That would be *most* ill-advised," said Dr. Muriel, cheerily. "The One Star Club—assuming it even exists—is supposed to be rather hush-hush."

"I'm not quite sure what it is, Muriel. Will you enlighten us?"

The door opened quietly as Nik Kovacevic and Maria slipped into the room. Maria was pushing a trolley with two bottles of white wine in coolers, eight wine glasses and three bowls of luxury mixed nuts. "My compliments," Nik murmured. "It's been a stressful day."

Maria parked the trolley and left the room, but Nik remained behind and fussed with the wine, opening and pouring it almost silently. Only Archie and Emily declined a melon-size glass of sauvignon blanc, and Nik compensated by putting the mixed nuts closest to them. He was nothing if not attentive to his guests. Though she didn't like him much, Emily was impressed by the way he looked after the RWGB committee personally, as though they were VIPs.

Dr. Muriel rested her right hand on the top of her cane and looked around at each of the group in turn, to be sure of holding their attention. She said, "The One Star Club is talked of in academic circles. A mythological group, if you will. It's said that its members join incognito, with enrollment only possible via a personal recommendation from one of the current members. If indeed it does exist, it seems it must be an international organization with a membership who meet occasionally in person, but otherwise conduct their business online."

"You're pulling our legs, Muriel," said Morgana, taking a large gulp of wine. "What business do they conduct, for goodness' sake?"

"Ah, well it's a business that would be of interest to you. That's why I thought you might have heard of it. In order to be a member of the One Star Club, one has to enjoy giving one-star reviews to products, services, books and films."

"I knew it!" said Cerys.

"A conspiracy?" said Archie. He shook his head, not convinced. He caught Emily's eye and shook his head again. As someone who was conspicuously taking notes, individual members of the committee automatically sought to persuade Emily to record their views.

"Surely not," said Polly. "What would be the point of it?"

"Mischief-making, score settling, sheer bloody-mindedness... Some have hypothesized that they're absurdists, others that they're anarchists trying to upset the cozy commerciality of unverifiable review systems."

"What makes you think that Winnie was anything to do with them?"

"I don't. I was merely asking the question."

"Her reviews were generally quite fair," said Morgana. Then, with a quick look at Cerys, "Generally."

"I don't bother much with reviews," said Zena.

"Never read them," said Archie.

"None of us does," said Morgana.

Polly caught Emily's eye and smiled as if to say, *I do.* Emily smiled and bent to her notes.

"A secret society?" said Cerys. "I'd love to know where they meet. I'd turn up and shake a bag of snakes in through the air-conditioning ducts to bite the lot of them."

Emily wrote *snakes*, struck by how specific this plan was, as if Cerys hadn't only just thought of it.

"Darling," said Morgana. "Imagine the trouble you'd have wrangling the snakes. Wouldn't they bite indiscriminately? What about the staff? What about the general public? What about you?"

"I'm not serious, M."

"I'm no convinced," said Archie. "About the One Star Club."

"No," said Morgana. "Me neither. No offense, Muriel."

"How do you know so much about it?" Zena asked. "You're not a member?"

"No indeed. Academics do have rather a sordid reputation for trashing each other's work, whether in the press or anonymously. But that's rather unjust. We're mostly very supportive of our colleagues."

"In layman's terms, Muriel's professional areas of interest encompass conundrums, puzzles and ethical considerations," said Morgana to Zena.

"You don't need to put it in layman's terms for me. Zena's as bright as the best of them." Zena made a huffing sound.

"Indeed." Dr. Muriel laughed her rattly laugh. "You know, I don't claim to be able to provide any answers. So I can only ask: could Winnie's appearance here be connected to the One Star Club, should such a club exist?"

"We invited her here," said Polly. "It doesn't make any sense—unless one of us is a member of this club."

Everyone looked around at each other, suspiciously.

"It takes me all day to write three pages of my manuscript," said Morgana. "Never mind the hours taken up with responsibilities associated with the RWGB. Where would I find the time to write unkind reviews of other people's books?"

"No need. You can leave that to the bloggers," said Cerys.

"Quite!" said Morgana. And then, realizing she had misspoken, she added, "Not that many of them succumb to the temptation, of course. Broadly, as you know, I'm in favor of bloggers."

"You mentioned that people could only join if they were recommended by a current member," said Polly. She took a sip of water—she was still very pale. "But what happens if someone wants to *leave* this club?"

"Ah!" said Zena. "Interesting."

"You think Winnie was killed because she tried to break ranks?" said Cerys, excitedly. "You think she might have been killed by other bloggers?" She stood and began to stride around the room, just as she would if she was trying to work through a difficult plot point while writing in her office at home. Realizing she was in company—and that she didn't want it to look as though she were responsible for this particular plot—she sat down again.

"We're certainly straying into the realms of fantasy, now," said Morgana. A slight tremor passed through her body, from hat to toe, betraying her nervousness.

"We're storytellers. Course it's tempting to try to put a story to the poor woman's death," said Archie. "But I cannae believe in this One Star Club. It's more likely a random killing, eh?"

"It looks as though more than one person was involved," said Emily. "At least two. It could have been a group effort."

"A group effort?" said Morgana. Another tremor, as if her body was rejecting the information that her mind had just taken in.

"You're not saying the police suspect the committee?" said Cerys. "We've all talked to them, haven't we? Ruled ourselves out. It's crazy. None of us could have done it." They looked around at each other again. And perhaps they realized that, although they knew each other, they didn't know each other's secrets.

"And then there's the poisoning," said Emily.

"Poisoning?" said Zena and Archie, more or less together. "What poisoning?"

"Cyanide," said Cerys.

"Oh," said Polly. "No, that was me. Overactive imagination, I think...Well, you know how it is. I'm OK now." She didn't look OK. She looked like a Victorian matchbox seller who has been out in the cold all night and hasn't had a decent meal in three weeks.

"Ach, well," said Archie. "You'd know if you'd been poisoned by cyanide."

"Who'd want to poison *you*, Polly?" said Zena, in a tone of voice that suggested she could think of a dozen people off the top of her head.

"I don't know. Some people are jealous."

"If Polly's in danger, we're all in danger, yeah? If it's about jealousy. We've all had our share of success." Zena's eyes went to Emily's notebook, to be sure she was writing that down.

Morgana said, "This is just the kind of speculation we need to avoid at the press conference. We need to say something nice about Winnie tonight and then cut it off there. What did we know of her, anyway?"

There was a polite, thoughtful silence. No one had known anything about her.

Zena took a purple lipstick out of her bag, removed the lid and twisted it before proffering it to Polly. "Here you are, Poll. Put a bit of color on."

Polly hesitated slightly but could hardly refuse without implying she thought that Zena had cold sores or germs. She applied the lipstick by feel, without the aid of a mirror. Now with purple lips, without a scrap of makeup on the rest of her face, she looked like a zombie in a YouTube video made by eleven-year-olds.

Cerys tried to help. She got out her blusher brush and a little pink pot. "This'll put roses in your cheeks, love." She stood and stroked the brush briskly down one side of Polly's face and then the other. Polly kept her face still and slid her eyes to the very left of her line of her vision to meet Emily's. Emily giggled. Zena now stood and began to apply purple eye shadow to Polly. As she and Cerys worked silently, competitively, to transform Polly into a crayon-faced monster, Morgana tried to get the meeting back on track.

"What shall I say about Winnie?"

Emily said, "Could you let her speak for herself by reading her competition entry?"

"Very good!" Morgana put on her glasses and looked through the papers in front of her on the table. "Yes, here it is. Winnie's effort is called 'The Secret.'"

"Ah," said Dr. Muriel. "Interesting."

"Oh dear. It seemed such an innocuous title, but now everything seems to connect to this One Star Club that you mentioned so (forgive me, Muriel) so mischievously just now."

Archie said: "Perhaps it's in code?"

Cerys snatched up the piece of paper. "I swear to you, M, I don't remember reading this or voting for it. There's something funny going on."

Zena put out her hand for the page, and Cerys put it in her hand. "Nuh. Never seen it." Zena looked around the table at her friends, puzzled and wary. "She writes about a star in the sky…One star! Morgana, what's going on?"

Archie said, "Ach. I was joking about the code. You know?"

Zena still had hold of Winnie's story. She tapped the page. "The universe has ways of communicating with us, and we can communicate with it, too. C'mon! We all know words are important. Every time we write something, *every time*, it's a kind of manifesto. It's heard. It's read. It gives a voice to what's inside our minds."

"Aye. Shopping lists an' all, Zena?"

"You want it. You think it. You write it. You buy it. Yeah? Shopping lists *work*. Kind of proves my point."

Morgana held up her hands. "Darlings, this is just the kind of lively debate we're all looking forward to at the conference tomorrow. That's why I so love it when we all get together. But, look, time's going on and we *have* to deal with the press conference." A worried little jingle of bracelets. "I'll investigate the selection and voting and whatnot when I get home. I'll need to contact an IT person, perhaps there's been a glitch. Never mind that now. The funniest—well, I mean the horriblest—thing that's happened is that poor Winnie has been murdered, and I need to say something about it. Death has cast its long and terrible shadow over the conference, and plucked one of our guests from our midst with cold, gray fingers… Is that too much?"

"Least it's all over and done with now, love," said Cerys. "No more death."

But she was wrong.

Nik Kovacevic had been at work since eight o'clock that morning, and he wouldn't finish before ten o'clock that night. Even if he'd been able to knock off early, he wouldn't have been able to rest. His mind was full of the day's events—they tumbled into his head like brightly-colored rubbish falling down a chute to be sorted. He picked through it all, piece by piece, trying to make sense of it. And, as if he was in the grip of a physical illness, he felt sudden flushes of anxiety every time it hit him that *one of his guests had died today.*

People died in hotels, of course they did. Life in a hotel was a more extravagant version of normal, everyday life. Shortly after someone wakes up in the morning, they get up and brush their teeth. At night, they will brush their teeth again and lie down on the bed to sleep. In between those two events, they breathe, eat, cry, laugh, talk, dress, get undressed, do their ablutions—and these things are universal, whether a person is at home in their flat in Notting Hill or staying at a hotel in Bloomsbury. At the Coram Hotel, the food cost more than it would at home. There was no housework to be done—or rather, none to be done by the guests. There was plenty to be done by the staff. There were clean cotton sheets on the bed and a chocolate placed on the pillow by Lydia or one of the other maids at night. There was fancy hand cream in the toilets and little hand towels that only need to be used once before they were washed. There was life. And sometimes there was death.

Some people die quietly, some die horribly. Fortunately, the poor lady who had died that day had been found in the grounds of the estate next door. That was something Nik Kovacevic was grateful for—even proud of. He understood the reason why a guest was prepared to pay a large sum of money to stay in an establishment like the Coram Hotel. It was because of the way life at the hotel *appeared* to be. The hotel had to seem like a lovely place to spend time (and money). He thought he might say something about it in his next staff meeting. He would explain that standards and services were important...no. All the staff knew that already. He would explain that they were magicians, creating an illusion. They earned their living in the gap between normal life and the life of ease offered at the hotel. And this gap was adjustable and illusory. Guests didn't want to pay for a gap that had dead bodies stuffed in it. He would say that. Or did it sound weird? It might be better to say nothing.

First there was a porter he needed to go and interview, whose papers were not quite in order. He needed to ensure that everything was sorted, one way or another, to the satisfaction of the Home Office. It was his duty to know everything that was going on in the hotel, and to forestall any potential trouble. When he'd been assistant manager here he'd intervened to stop illegal, high-stakes gambling meetings, organized prostitution (the disorganized kind was tolerated, so long as it was discreet) and too much drug taking among staff (a little bit of cocaine use among chefs was known to help them get through the long working hours, though too much made them belligerent; and the use of expensive drugs by lower-grade staff was not a good idea, because they couldn't afford it). After he had dealt with the porter, he had to be on hand at the RWGB press conference, to ensure the hotel was portrayed in the best possible light. Though if anyone said anything unfavorable, he was not sure what he was supposed to do. Turn off the lights? Charge to the front with a roar and threaten everyone? Stay silent and fume? Probably the latter. That's what he usually did.

Nik walked purposefully on his way to his office from the Captain Thomas Coram room, straightening things that didn't need straightening, nodding to staff, enjoying being in charge. He tried not to eavesdrop when he went into meeting rooms. But four words repeated by the occupants of the last one he'd visited had reached his consciousness and now tangled themselves around his other thoughts: the One Star Club. What was that?

CHAPTER NINE
CITIZEN JOURNALIST

The door of the Captain Thomas Coram room slammed open and Teena burst in, her jaw pushed slightly forward in belligerent triumph. Emily saw the ripple of mild panic go round the room. The members of the committee were trying to assess how it might look to an outsider that they were sitting there gulping expensive white wine, and eating an assortment of fancy nuts, in the aftermath of a woman's death. Not good, from the guilty-schoolgirl looks on their faces.

"I know what's happened!" Teena said.

"Yes," said Morgana soothingly. "Yes, of course." Clearly she had no idea what Teena was on about.

"I've worked it out."

Teena wanted the committee members to ask her what she had worked out, and because they found her rather annoying, everyone politely resisted.

Cerys folded first, perhaps because she was a grandmother and used to this sort of thing. "You want to come in and tell us what's going on, love?"

Teena came in and sat down. "I'll have some of that wine, if you don't mind. See, in my line of work—"

"Local council?" asked Polly, sweetly, pouring her a glass.

"Citizen journalist. I'm used to digging about, finding facts."

"Of course you are. How wonderful!" Morgana was at her most soothing again.

"I've been up there. I've worked it out. She was pushed, wasn't she?"

"Winnie? Was she?" The silver bangles jingled around Morgana's weak-looking wrists. If Winnie had been pushed by someone in this room, it was unlikely to have been Morgana.

"Yes."

"Been up where?" Polly's patient sweetness would have worked much better without the scary face paint.

"Teena, darling, have you told the police?" Morgana asked warily.

"I spoke to that young one. He was very rude."

Everyone cheered up at this. Zena spoke for the group. "What'd he say, babes?"

"He said he was thinking of opening an outreach service for amateur sleuths."

Dr. Muriel treated them to a longish, staccato version of her laugh. Emily didn't even smile.

"Nuts?" said Polly, offering the bowl to Teena. Emily smiled at that.

"No thanks, Polly. I'm going up there again to have a look." Teena drained her glass.

"Up where?" Polly persisted.

"The roof garden."

"Darling, have you talked to anyone else about this?" Morgana was worried, as always, about how to contain the information and stop it reaching the press.

"No."

Polly said, "How did you know about the roof terrace?"

"Well, I asked the hotel manager."

"So you've told the policeman and the hotel manager?"

"And Maggie."

Polly stood up. "You need to be careful. You might be in danger. I'll come with you if you like."

"I got the idea when we did that writing exercise, Polly. I wrote about Winnie's death from the point of view of the murderer. I could see my hands closing round her throat, and then pushing her off so she landed several stories below and broke all her bones. It was really vivid."

"I've missed a bit," said Cerys. "Who's the murderer? Is it Teena?"

"Darling, it's fiction. Teena's so clever she's imagined it all." Morgana only hesitated for a moment. "Haven't you?"

"Yeah. I don't know who killed Winnie. But I know how they did it. If I go up to the roof garden, can you go and stand underneath, Polly? There's some bins round by the kitchen. I need to see if there's room for you to lie in one of them."

"Polly's going to go and lie in a bin?" Zena looked as though she'd just been told it was Christmas and she was allowed to open her presents early. "Praps we should all come and look?"

"Darlings, no. We're out of time. We *really* need to go next door. Polly will look after Teena."

"Polly, love, if you're playing nursemaid, you might want to pop to the loo first." Cerys made a wiping motion in front of her face. "Tidy yourself up a bit."

The group began to rise. Nothing useful had been decided. Emily had made lots of notes and yet there was nothing that seemed interesting or relevant. She thought she really ought to explain that she'd already worked out some of what had happened to Winnie. "Listen, Teena—"

"That's all right, Emily. Me and Polly've got this."

Emily let it go. She didn't want to look as if she was trying to compete; as if she was jealous that Polly and Teena were going off together to investigate.

Cerys spoke kindly to Teena. "She wasn't found in the bins, love. You do realize that?"

Before Teena could get a word in, Zena spoke for her: "She could have been moved, Cee. Couple of blokes working together. They wrap her up in a carpet, bundle her body onto the estate."

"Ah! Like Cleopatra being delivered to the feet of the great Antony." Morgana knew that Zena liked to keep no more than two steps away from the Cleopatra myth. "Was there a carpet found by the body?"

There was a tiny pause while Zena thought about this. "Couple of blokes and no carpet, then."

Teena looked pointedly at Cerys and Zena, standing side by side. Next to fragile Morgana and frail Polly, they looked beefy. "Could have been a couple of big women."

Cerys was good-humored about it. "Or one big woman. Fair play, there's many a wife has to haul her husband out of the pub single-handed round my neck of the woods." Not that Cerys herself had ever had to do it. "But who would have wanted to push Winnie to her death in the first place? Beats me."

Archie spoke softly. "There are dark thoughts in the minds of many men."

"And women," said Teena. In a room of people used to getting the last word, she had done well to win this one. And, by the expression on her face, she knew it. She couldn't have looked any more smug if someone had taken Zena's purple lipstick and written SMUG right across her forehead. It was too bad she wouldn't live long enough to enjoy it.

CHAPTER TEN
NIK AND HENRI

Nik slipped into the chair behind his desk and undid his suit jacket—a few minutes' comfort while he was out of the public eye, so long as he remembered to do it up again—then pressed a button on his computer to take it out of sleep mode.

There was a scribbled message on the pad on his desk by Jurgen, the head of security, and he read it as his computer sparked into life.

> Need to speak to you URGENTLY, Nik. Scruffy-looking members of the public wandering about the hotel, saying they're here for VIGIL. They're alarming the paying guests. THE CORAM HOTEL IS NOT A HOSTEL. J.

Jurgen's job was to be suspicious of everyone, and slightly intimidating in a subtle and superficially courteous way. He certainly intimidated Nik, though Nik tried not to show it. He put the message to one side as Henri the porter came to the door.

Nik didn't ask Henri to sit down. He said, "Cyril's been spotted here. Do you know anything about it?"

"Cyril?" Henri tried to look mystified; he frowned and looked upward, as though searching his memory for clues. His standard of acting wouldn't have got him selected for the part of a tree in a school nativity play. But Henri wasn't auditioning. He was playing for time. He knew who Cyril was. He and Cyril hailed from the same country of origin and they were friends.

"Cyril Loman. He mustn't come here. Understand, Henri? There's police here, investigating that other matter. Loyalty's important, yes. Friends help each other. I know that. You know it. But if Cyril attracts their attention…"

"Cyril visit the ladies of the conference."

"You *have* seen him, then?"

Henri stared at Nik. This was one of those interviews where one person holds all the power and already knows the answers to the questions—and Nik was that person. Nik didn't want information, he wanted to make a point. Henri stood still and waited to discover what point Nik wanted to make. Henri had no authority or influence. He did a job that earned him minimum wage, and he lived quietly, using the money he earned to support his wife and two small children. He was a long, long way from his country of origin. But every morning, as he left for work dressed in his striped waistcoat and smart black trousers, he gave thanks for the mildness of the British weather and the tolerance of British people, and every now and then he offered up a little prayer on behalf of the British justice system, whose close attention he hoped to avoid.

Nik turned the screen of his computer so that Henri could see it. He tapped a button on his keyboard a couple of times, quickly, so that it made a satisfying knitting needle clickety-click. Henri watched a replay of CCTV images of his friend Cyril Loman heaving a black bin bag over the wall between the hotel and the estate.

"You realize this is stealing?" said Nik. He sat back in his chair and folded his arms, and did his serious face.

Henri gawped and then, he couldn't help it, he could feel a smile lick his expression, and then it burned up his face from cheeks to eyes as rapidly as if someone had put a match to a photograph. He tried to get a grip on himself—he literally put his arms around himself and hugged his ribs—but it was no good. He was struck with mirth, a naughty boy in the headmaster's office at school. The memory this prompted, of relatively carefree days as a schoolboy back home, only made him feel more joyful. He shook with silent laughter. Stealing? From a rubbish bin? Really? It was the kind of wild story a grandmother would tell children to illustrate the folly of a rich man. That thought sobered him—he'd heard his grandmother had died a few years ago, but he'd never had the chance to say goodbye—and the reminder of his lost relatives made him feel sad…and he was then happy again. He couldn't help it. Stealing! He giggled unmanfully, unable to stop himself.

"Henri, pull yourself together, mate. You're a giggling buffoon."

But it would be three or four minutes before Henri managed to regain control and explain to Nik Kovacevic how those conference ladies had insulted his friend Cyril Loman and besmirched his honor, and how the furious M. Loman had decided to respond.

"No more of this nonsense, you understand? If the police get wind of any of it…"

Henri's face snapped back to its default expression. Fear smothered his mirth. "I help for loyalty. Is OK, Nik? I cannot danger. I cannot."

"Yeah, mate. It's OK. I won't let anything happen to you. No danger. If anyone comes sniffing about—police or Home Office or whatever—I should get wind of it. I'll be able to warn you. Until then, keep your nose out of trouble. Cyril can help with the papers. He's all well and good with the shortcuts and circumventing bureaucracy. But he can't help at the other end of it. You can't just bribe your way out of trouble if you tangle with the police in this country."

Henri couldn't follow all this. Sniffing, wind, nose, *what*? But he followed the important parts: police, Home Office, trouble, Cyril, papers.

Outside the office, Emily Castles lurked. She knew that Nik would be going to the press conference, and she had hoped she might be able to go through his office looking for clues—incriminating CCTV footage, something like that (she only had his word for it that it was being rebooted earlier that day). But when she arrived, she saw that he was still in the office and he wasn't alone. She stood and listened. Her behavior would have got her a warning if she'd been a member of Nik Kovacevic's staff and he'd caught her at it. But she wasn't and he didn't. She heard the tail end of the conversation:

"The upshot, Henri, is that I have CCTV showing you and Cyril putting something heavy over the wall."

"CCTV not filming!"

"It wasn't filming, and now it is. That's the nature of CCTV. It's there to film things. You can't have it turned off for too long, or it triggers an alarm. And what do I see when I review this afternoon's footage? Just about the most incriminating footage possible, given what happened earlier today, of two men manhandling what might well be a woman's body in a bin bag."

"Cyril honor. Reputation. He ask me."

"Well, I gathered that. I don't intend showing it to anyone. All I'm saying is, you need to keep quiet about the other matter. Keep it zipped. Understand?"

Henri didn't really understand. The only things he generally kept zipped were his trousers and his tracksuit tops. "Is dangerous?"

"Not if you keep your head. I'm going to press delete on this. See?" There was a pause in the conversation, suggesting that Nik and Henri were watching the image disappear from the screen. "Don't do anything else silly. Go on, off with you."

Hearing those words, Emily scarpered and hid behind a tall, wing-backed chair in a corner of the lobby. She watched as Henri left the office and went back to work. Even if Emily could have listened inside his head, she wouldn't have understood. He was thinking in French, his mother tongue. He was wondering how he was going to explain to his wife that it didn't matter where you went, you always got asked to help someone do something in order to make their life easier, and sometimes it just made your life much worse. And how, though he'd repaid a debt to Nik Kovacevic a few hours ago, suddenly he was in his debt all over again.

Nik Kovacevic picked up the phone and called Jurgen. And then he made his way to the press conference.

Seeing Nik walk by from where she stood admiring a stopped clock on a mantelpiece, half-hidden by the chair, Emily doubled back into his office. She had a few minutes, that was all, and then she'd have to get to the press conference herself. How should she spend the time? She pulled at the drawers on the filing cabinets in the office, but they were all locked. She puzzled briefly over the chart on the wall labeled Rubbish Champion, with a blank square under each month of the year, where a passport-size photo was supposed to go. What was she looking for? A signed confession? A bottle of poison?

The computer was still on. Perhaps it would yield his secrets. Emily opened the CCTV window and looked at nothing much happening outside. She opened the latest website Nik had looked at: a hotel review site. She had a fairly good idea what he'd been up to on there. It might prove he was sneaky, but it didn't make him a murderer. What should she be looking for? What should she be doing? A computer is no different from any other oracle. The answers it gives are only as good as the questions asked.

Emily pulled out her notebook, hoping that something she had written would prompt her to ask the right question. What did she want to know? She realized there was something that was bothering her, though perhaps Nik didn't know the answer. But for a few minutes she had the world's finest minds at her fingertips, if she cared to summon them. It seemed daft to waste the opportunity. She opened the search box on the computer's Internet browser and typed: *What is the antidote to cyanide poisoning?*

CHAPTER ELEVEN
THE PRESS CONFERENCE

Emily arrived in the T. S. Eliot suite just as the press conference was about to start. As she took her place next to Dr. Muriel, she leaned over and whispered, "I've got a bone to pick with you."

Dr. Muriel folded her arms and looked amused. She thrived on argument.

"There's no such thing as the One Star Club, is there?"

"Ha! I suppose there *could* be such a thing."

"But if there were, it would be a wild coincidence, wouldn't it? Because you've just made it up."

Dr. Muriel grinned. "Ah, Emily. It's impossible to hoodwink you."

"But why say it, if it's not true?" Dr. Muriel's methods ran counter to what Emily understood about how science worked.

"I find it instructive to see how people react to such stories. One has so little control over 'real' information. Who can say what is the truth? Who 'owns' the truth? So it can be useful to look at how a person reacts to a hypothetical, i.e. a 'truth' that the story-teller owns. I call it evaluating by theorizing."

Whereas Emily might have called it *making things up*.

"You see, by looking at a person's reaction to the hypothetical, about which one knows a great deal (having created it), one hopes to understand that person's likely reaction to a real situation, about which one knows next to nothing."

Dr. Muriel seemed very pleased with the way things had gone in the Captain Thomas Coram room. But Emily wasn't so sure. "I hope it doesn't provoke anyone into doing something rash."

"That would be most unfortunate."

"I don't see how anyone in that room could be responsible for Winnie's death, do you? There was no motive."

"No, indeed. I should think the temporary boost for book sales and the press attention for the conference was entirely unintentional."

"Ladies and gentlemen," called Morgana from the table at the front. "I think we might begin, don't you?"

There was a shushing and settling in their seats as everyone got ready to listen to what she had to say. The shushing was more for the enjoyment of doing it than for any need to quiet a rowdy crowd. Attendance at the press conference was sparse. Four rows of chairs had been set up facing a table at the front, but there were plenty of places available—apparently there were hotter tickets on a Saturday night in Central London.

Morgana Blakely stood behind the table, looking nervous but brave, like a shy celebrity who has been asked to take part in a game show in aid of charity. She had accessorized a flouncy, knee-length black dress with a pale-pink cashmere shrug and a jaunty pink fez. She caught Emily's eye and smiled, but there was no sunshine in the smile—it was more of a wince. Emily and Dr. Muriel sat in the second row. Zena sat next to Cerys in the first row. Trevor was there, but Zena had taken care to place herself some distance from him, as if there was impropriety in sitting next to a reporter at a press conference.

Emily leaned back in her seat to see who else was there. Nik Kovacevic was standing by the door at the back of the room, with his hands folded in front of him. Maggie was sitting in the fourth row at the back, handbag on her lap. There was no sign of Teena, Polly or Archie.

Members of the public were not supposed to have been admitted, but the people who were here for the vigil had been allowed in. They were being indulged. Their "grief" was their trump card, even though it was a manufactured grief for someone they hadn't known.

"These are the sort of people," whispered Dr. Muriel, a little too loudly, "for whom TV talent shows and celebrity Twitter feeds have more meaning than events in their own lives. They have forgotten how to live for themselves. They have forgotten how to interact with others."

Emily agreed. There were several middle-aged people in the audience who reminded her of women she had met in temp jobs over the years, of whom colleagues had whispered without irony or censure, "She's never been the same since Diana died." In Emily's experience, people like this overlooked the small sputtering victories and disappointments that weaved in and out of their daily lives, which were apparently meaningless to them. Though they were ordinary themselves, they rejected anything around them that was ordinary. There had to be a divorce, a death, a rags-to-riches story with a narrative arc, to deserve their attention and empathy. If it hadn't been written by a storyliner on a soap opera or a reality TV show, they didn't understand its relevance to their lives.

She whispered to Dr. Muriel, "I think they're expecting to listen to Morgana's speech and make simple choices—yes/no; good/bad; naughty/nice; winner/loser; forgiven/condemned."

"Ah! Like a live studio audience for the press conference?"

"Shush!" someone said from the front row.

Morgana began, "I would like to welcome you to the Coram Hotel on behalf of the Romance Writers of Great Britain. I should begin by explaining to newcomers and members of the press that we are in no way affiliated to the Romance Authors of America, the Romance Writers of the United Kingdom, the Romance Novelists' Association…"

Emily looked around, trying to identify the members of the press among the audience. There were two people with notebooks open on their laps. One was Trevor, who looked over at Zena every now and then, leading Emily to deduce correctly that he was her contact from the *Ham & High*. The other was a middle-aged white man wearing heavy-rimmed glasses with thick lenses. Neither man wrote anything down as Morgana droned on about the RWGB and the purpose of the annual conference: "For a few wonderful days, we bring romance writers together from all over the country to celebrate our art, our passion: writing. For a few days, we are not alone at our computers: we can laugh and share with one another the joy we get from writing stories that make the heart sing."

Dr. Muriel nudged Emily and whispered, "Those people from the blogathon room? What would you call them?"

"Vigilants?" suggested Emily.

"Looking at the expressions on their faces, the vigilants seem to have certain strong feelings: *Winnie did not deserve to die*, and *You are the bad people who brought her here.*"

"So long as Morgana keeps her speech simple and easy to follow, some of them might change their minds."

But Emily was worried for Morgana. She was going to try and charm everyone. She would use rhetorical devices to appeal for sympathy. She would be subtle and low-key. She would be self-deprecating and apologetic. Any confession of guilt would be taken at face value, as a confession of guilt rather than a polite shouldering of the burden of responsibility as host of this conference. Emily watched a lot of television, and she enjoyed reality programs. She knew that Morgana needed to break down and cry—a really wailing, mucusy cry would be best—and allow herself to be built up again by the intervention of a third party if she wanted the sympathy of the bystanders in the audience. Morgana might be able to appeal to the members of the press with her fancy speech but, so far as Emily could see, there were only two of them, and Trevor would be looking for a local story, and the other chap…he might not even be a member of the press. He could be sitting there waiting for inspiration to write a haiku in his notebook for all Emily knew.

Morgana said, "I'd like to read an excerpt from a piece of Winnie's writing that will give an insight into what a special woman she was." Everyone looked disappointed. Not knowing that they'd have preferred it if she'd tossed aside the paper she was reading from and started to cry, Morgana looked perplexed but carried on. This was about Winnie, right? This was a tribute?

Emily knew Morgana wanted to say the right thing. She still hadn't understood that it wasn't about Winnie. She was on trial. Nobody cared *what* she said, they cared *how* she said it. Dignity and composure shown by a woman in the aftermath of a tragedy was usually interpreted as a sign of guilt. If they had been furnished with a piece of apparatus with voting buttons, Emily thought that several of the vigilants would have pressed the guilty button by now.

"Dear Winnie was a member of our family…" This was better. The vigilants perked up. Families were dysfunctional and prone to shouting. They harbored secrets. Or they did on TV, anyway. This might not be too dull, after all.

The heavy wooden door at the back of the room opened and closed with a bang. Morgana paled, as if she had seen a ghost. Emily turned to see whether Nik Kovacevic would try to bar the newcomer's way. But he was no longer at the door. Perhaps he'd decided he had better things to do than listen to platitudes.

At first Emily couldn't place the man who came in, though she felt she recognized him from somewhere. He had a brick-shaped face, short, graying hair, and a neat mustache. And he had the shocked look of a man who has just encountered a moderately dangerous wild animal, though the most dangerous wild animal in Britain was a badger, and there were precious few of them in Bloomsbury.

Then Emily realized where she knew the man from: she had seen his photo on Winnie's tribute page. Though Winnie herself, like many women, was thinner in some photos, plumper in others, and had experimented with a variety of hairstyles, Des Kraster looked almost exactly the same in real life as he did in his wedding photo, though his hair was now slightly grayer.

Emily looked at Morgana and saw that she recognized him, too. As Des found a seat in the fourth row, blinking and breathing unevenly, Emily saw that the poor man was trying not to cry. This had the effect of making her eyes fill up with tears. Looking around, she could see that others were similarly affected. Tears are even more infectious than yawns or smiles when a man is trying not to cry in a room full of women.

Standing behind the table at the front of the room, Morgana made her hand into a fist and brought it in front of her mouth, but she was unable to stifle the mewling sound that came from it. Her nose ran, and tears ran from her eyes.

The strangers in the room saw it, and they forgave her.

CHAPTER TWELVE
PANDEMONIUM

Des looked around at the rather lovely meeting room and wondered about the people who had gathered—so he understood—to say something about his wife's death. It was weird to think of all these famous novelists sitting here ready to speak up for Winnie (Des had no reason to think that the audience comprised anyone else, and had been somewhat misled about the purpose of the press conference by the Reception staff at the hotel, in good faith, since they had little enough idea why it had been arranged themselves).

Des wouldn't have been able to say with any truthfulness that he had dreamed of visiting London with Winnie—he'd rather have gone to Las Vegas any day of the week. And it was no man's dream to travel anywhere at short notice to make arrangements to repatriate his wife's body. But Des had been touched to learn, as he checked in to the hotel around half an hour ago, that the room he would be staying in had been paid for by the committee of RWGB. He felt kindly toward this classy-sounding lady in her pink furry outfit standing at the front of the Captain Thomas Coram room with snot dripping out of her nose, not realizing that he was simply benefitting from the Coram Hotel's rather draconian cancellation policy, having been shown to the bedroom that had been reserved for Winnie's stay.

Des was exhausted. He noticed the weepy eyes of some of the audience members turned toward him and guessed they recognized him from the wedding photograph on the tribute site, which he had seen. He shrank from the attention. He had no way of knowing that the glamour these people associated with the recently bereaved made it impossible for them to resist staring at him. He hoped that something might happen to get them all to look elsewhere. He got his wish.

It happened like this. First of all, from somewhere outside, there was a prolonged squawking sort of a sound. No one noticed it above the honking of traffic until it drew nearer and got louder: the thick brick walls of the hotel had been built to keep the outside out. But then the windows briefly darkened as a flying object passed by on its downward trajectory. Screams and shouts of horror came from three smokers standing by the railings outside the Captain Thomas Coram room. Passersby stopped in the street to look. The members of the audience at the press conference stood and made for the door or the window. Pandemonium ensued.

CHAPTER THIRTEEN
PRINCESS HOITY-TOITY

There are some people who run from trouble and some who run toward it. Though it wasn't yet clear what had happened, many people instinctively tried to run from the room, to get away from danger as quickly as possible. They feared some kind of terrorist attack. Then someone near the window shouted "Teena! It's Teena!" and people started to gather there to look. There was no way to get to the window to see for herself, so Emily realized she had to get outside and see what was going on.

It seemed melodramatic to run—whatever had happened, had happened, and running outside wasn't going to help. But Emily wanted to get there quickly. She couldn't walk at a normal pace. So she scuttled. She bustled. As she walked down the steps that led up to the hotel, and saw the street outside that she had left only that morning, it seemed as if a year must have passed. The light had altered because it was now evening, and the rain had stopped, so the quality of the air was lighter and fresher, and it seemed a different place. The most different thing about it, though, was that there was a woman's body impaled on the spikes of the ornate black railings outside the hotel. The woman was dead. The woman was Teena.

Det. Rory James was there. An ambulance arrived, siren squealing, and parked up next to the hotel with blue lights flashing. The paramedics went to work on Teena, still lying face-up on the railings.

Two uniformed policemen drew up in a squad car and immediately set about trying to keep onlookers away.

Emily tried to get close to Det. James. "Polly!" she said. "Is Polly all right? Where's Polly?"

He said, "I need you to leave now. If you recognize anyone here, take them with you."

"What happened to Teena? Did she fall?"

"Emily, I can't tell you anything. You need to clear the area."

"She thought Winnie fell from the roof terrace. She went up to see."

"Ms. Durani shouldn't have been up there. I'll need to talk to you later. We don't want any more accidents. You see what happens when members of the public take it upon themselves to get involved in police investigations?"

There was no sign of Polly. Emily went back inside the hotel and dialed Polly's mobile phone, but it went straight to voice mail. She went to the elevator and stood there waiting, feeling slightly panicky. What if something had happened to Polly?

Emily thought to herself (as she sometimes thought in moments of stress), *What would Jessie do?* Jessie was her golden retriever who had died of old age a few months before. The answer, of course, was that if Jessie were alive she would go and sniff round by the bins in the hope of finding a bit of leftover sausage to eat. Emily had no intention of doing that. Still, thinking about Jessie calmed her. The elevator was taking forever! She had to do something. She had to go somewhere. She went to the bins.

The stinky courtyard was so repellent to her, and yet now so familiar, that Emily was like a newly married princess in a cautionary fairy tale—the hoity-toity kind of princess who returns one day to her humble childhood home and gets her comeuppance after complaining about the smell in the pigsty. She would have found it funny to think of her visit to the bins as her "homecoming" if she wasn't agitated and slightly in shock. Two deaths and an attempted poisoning—what next? She had a horrible image of Polly and Teena tussling, of the two of them falling, one in one direction, one in the other. She hardly dared imagine what she might find here. Would M. Loman and Henri the porter be heaving Polly's body, in a black plastic sack, out of a yellow or red bin and putting it over the wall?

But no, there she was, alive and well, holding the long stub of a menthol cigarette and looking reasonably cheerful, which suggested she had no idea what had happened. "I know, I know! I shouldn't be smoking. Don't judge me. I've been waiting here for ages for Teena."

"Teena..." said Emily. She cleared her throat unnecessarily. "Teena..."

"She's gone up to the roof in one of those slow, old elevators."

"And she's come down again, a great deal faster."

"Emily?" Polly could see there was something wrong; that Emily was being a bit peculiar. "Are you OK?"

"Teena's dead!"

Polly looked up toward the roof terrace as if she doubted Emily's word, and expected to be able to point out Teena to her. Emily looked as well. They saw a uniformed police officer come to the fence and look down.

"But how?" said Polly. "What on earth—someone's gone up there? They attacked her? Or...no, you said she'd come back down again."

"She fell. She fell onto the railings at the front. I saw her. It was horrible."

"Ugh, you look as though you're going to faint. Let's go inside." Polly put the stub of her cigarette carefully into her handbag. "I can't believe…God, it's terrible. Teena was with me just a little while ago, right as rain."

Emily thought, maybe it wasn't Teena! Maybe there had been a mistake and everything was OK? And then she knew she was being irrational, and she was in shock. She had seen Teena's dead body right there in front of her, only five minutes ago.

"What about the press conference?" asked Polly as they reached the bar. Morgana, Dr. Muriel, Cerys and Zena were already in there, drinking white wine as if it was going out of fashion. Archie was at the mirrored bar, watching himself trying to order a cranberry juice.

"What?" said Emily.

"The press conference. Did they have to call it off?"

"Everyone pretty much lost interest when Teena's body sailed past the window and impaled on the railings outside. I don't think we'll be getting a write-up in the *Ham & High*."

"Darlings," Morgana called. "Come and have some wine. Were you up there with her, Polly? Did you see what happened?"

"She went up to the roof terrace. I went to the loo, had a bit of a tidy-up." Polly had indeed scrubbed the purple and pink off her face and lips. "Then I was supposed to wait for her by the bins—you know that courtyard near the kitchen? She had this theory that Winnie's body had landed there, and it had been moved. She was going to call down, I was supposed to look up. It was all nonsense, really, or so I supposed. I mean, no one knows what happened to Winnie except the person who killed her." Polly paused then. The other members of the committee were nodding, taking it all in. "I couldn't understand why Teena was suddenly the expert investigator. It's my fault, isn't it? For getting her to try and imagine some event in her life and see it from another side. I didn't think she'd choose to write about Winnie's death. Anyway, I went outside. I kept looking up, I didn't see her. And then Emily came and found me."

"It's a blessed relief you didn't see her fall, love," said Cerys.

"I must have just missed it. It took rather a long time to scrub that lot off my face."

"I think a vision like that would stay with me for the rest of my life. Haunt my nightmares." Cerys shook her head sadly.

"Aye, it would." Archie had a blurry look in his eyes, as if he couldn't shake off his nightmares even when he was awake...

"Babes." Zena's imagination had taken flight, she could feel it fluttering in her head. "You're not saying Teena killed Winnie?"

"No, why would she do that?"

"What if she pushed her off, yeah, and then she was going to lure you up there and push you off?"

"Darling, you have such a wonderful imagination. It's what makes you such a fine novelist. But Teena didn't strike me as flamboyant enough to commit murder. Or strong enough." Morgana glugged her wine. "And anyway why would anyone want to kill Polly? That's just absurd."

Zena looked as if she could think why someone might want to kill Polly, but Cerys spoke first. "So they both fell? Nasty accidents, then, if you ask me. Least it's over now. I'll be glad to get back to Wales, mind. I've had enough of this now."

"I wonder if we should cancel the conference. For decency's sake, we should. But we'll never be able to get hold of tonight's dinner guests in time. Half of them will be on their way here in a cab by now. Not together. Separate cabs. Oh! I'm squiffy. No more wine for me. If you see me drink another drop, shoot me."

"Ah." Dr. Muriel looked around at the group. "An interesting conundrum. If Morgana asks to be shot, is it OK to shoot her?"

"I don't think so," said Emily, alarmed.

"At least we know your wretched One Star Club has nothing to do with it." Morgana signaled to the barman for another bottle of wine.

Zena's imagination was still flying free. "Jumping from a roof for no reason is exactly what members of secret societies do."

"I don't think Muriel was suggesting it was that kind of secret society. More like a malign version of a shopping reward club or a professional association." Morgana dug in her purse and scattered several credit-card-size pieces of plastic on the table in front of her, testifying to her non-malign membership of the Society of Authors, the Writers' Guild of Great Britain, the Romance Writers of Great Britain, Sainsbury's Nectar Rewards, Tesco's Clubcard and the Automobile Association Breakdown service. "I mean none of these, you see, require anyone to jump off the roof after sign-up." She hiccuped.

"I think you should cancel," said Archie.

Morgana stared at him, aghast, before realizing he wasn't talking about canceling all her cards, he was talking about the conference. She was still slightly aghast, but much less confused. "You may be right. Poor Des Kraster. Poor Winnie. Poor Teena. I'm not sure what to do."

"I agree it's bordering on disrespect, M, but it's even more disrespectful to invite people here tonight, and then when they turn up, you send them away hungry again. I'm not saying that if we throw food at the problem, it'll go away—Lord knows I've tried it myself often enough over the years." Cerys patted her thighs. "I'm testament to the fact it doesn't work. But we can all get together and commemorate, see?"

Morgana had gathered up her cards and was having difficulty trying to fit them back in her wallet. She closed one eye, which seemed to make things a bit easier. "What would the Romance Writers of the UK do? Or the LGBT Romance Writers? I don't want our members making the comparison and finding us callous."

"Their events are far too popular to be able to cancel at short notice, love—too many people coming in from all over the country."

"All over the world," said Zena. "Didn't the RWUK have Nelson Mandela for their centenary?"

"Last summer party the LGBT lot had was onboard a ship by Tower Bridge. Dame Judi Dench, boombangaboom cocktails, goodie bags from Asprey's, fireworks. No expense spared."

"Cerys!" Morgana was flushed, though it might have been the wine. "You didn't go?"

"Had to. Invited by a school friend. Would have seemed rude not to. Mind, it's windy up on deck. Had my picture taken perched on a cannon between Daniel Craig and Sir Ian McKellen. That was a three cans of hairspray event, and no mistake." Cerys patted her helmet of hair at the back and trembled slightly at the memory, though whether it was at the horror of her hairdo being blown out of place, or the thrill of being wedged between those two actors, she didn't say.

"Ach, who cares about them? We could join their organizations if we wanted to, but we don't want to. It's what's happened here, to us, to our people, that's disturbing. We can't just serve canapés and drink white wine," (Archie himself wasn't drinking it) "and pretend it never occurred."

Dr. Muriel tapped her cane on the ground, very gently, to get everyone's attention. "I could tackle the subject tomorrow, as part of my ethics in literature talk. That way, everyone gets to air their opinions, without anyone feeling the decision has been taken lightly, with no respect for the dead. You'll have a chance to explain why you haven't canceled."

"Muriel, you are so considerate. Will we start with your session, then? I'd planned to begin with Zena's talk on racial characterizations in literature."

"Sounds interesting, Zena."

"Yeah, I'm pleading the case for a more varied description of black skin on the page. Gotta be possible to go beyond using confectionery as a comparison. 'Chocolate this' and 'caramel that.' Yeah, OK! I'm with you! But that's not all there is."

"It's a marvelous topic," Morgana agreed. "Do you mind if we move it after the break?"

"I don't mind, babes. If we're not talking confectionery, Muriel, then it's wood: ebony, mahogany, teak—"

"I'll put you on at eleven, then. And, Muriel, yours'll be on first thing. I must make a fuss of poor Maggie, tomorrow. We've invited her all the way here, and she'll have expected to be feted, and we've ignored her. She's such a sweet, quiet little thing with that slightly down-beaten look, as though life's been nibbling away at her, the way she nibbles away at those fingernails. Where is she? Any idea, Emily?"

"I'm not sure. Everyone scattered when they realized Teena had died."

"Perhaps we ought not to lose sight of her."

"Well," Emily admitted, "I don't think she'd be stupid enough to go up to the roof terrace, but they do say bad news comes in threes."

"Oh, I doubt she's in danger. I just mean, given all that's happened, I hope she's not blogging it."

Polly twisted in her seat and looked around the bar. "I thought I saw her in here just now...There she is! In the corner, look—with Winnie's husband."

Morgana stood and waved for them to join her. After a brief whispered conversation, Maggie picked up her handbag and walked over. Des nodded politely to the committee, and left the bar.

Morgana fetched a chair for Maggie and fussed over her, pouring her a glass of wine.

Maggie said, "Des couldn't face company just now. Nothing personal. He doesn't blame you."

"Of course not. I'm not surprised. I think if I'd have been in his situation, I'd have skedaddled. And what must you be feeling? These aren't the best circumstances to make your debut among the Romance Writers of Great Britain."

Maggie gripped her handbag. "I suppose it means I'm the winner now, with the other two gone?"

CHAPTER FOURTEEN
THE GALA DINNER

It was time for the gala dinner, though nobody much felt like celebrating. Even the vigil had fizzled out. Emily had a quick wash and brush-up and then looked into the Brunswick room. Des was in there, a chair pulled up to the table with the wilting, plastic-wrapped flowers and the stuffed toy cats underneath. He was staring at the scrolling tributes on the computer screen in front of him, and he was alone except for the couple in the blue anoraks. They sat side by side, staring straight ahead of them at nothing at all, taking it in turns to dip their hands into a family pack of prawn cocktail crisps, with the synchronicity honed in a long marriage.

No one had proposed holding a vigil for Teena. First, she lacked the intrinsic glamour that was Winnie's birthright as an American who had lived in the blessed land of movies, New York, and Disney World. Second, it appeared that Teena had died while sticking her nose in where it frankly didn't belong, and nobody ever held a vigil for something like that. Third, even the most rabid proponents of public grief can get compassion fatigue. Teena's death was where this lot drew the line. Her death seemed to have deflated them, suggesting as it did that people just keep on dying no matter what anyone tries to do about it. Fourth, it had all seemed a bit too real and ugly: many of them had been at the press conference and seen Teena's dead body through the window of the T. S. Eliot room. Many now felt they had done their bit and hadn't returned to the

Captain Thomas Coram room. Of those who did return, many had got hungry and drifted back home to have dinner and watch TV. Frazer the bookseller had packed up and gone. Only the anorak couple were still here, dining on crisps.

Emily went over to Des. "How are you doing, Des? Do you want to come and join us? We're going to have dinner. Morgana was going to say a few words about your wife."

He shook his head. "The police say they're keeping an open mind. Is that Britspeak for 'we know what happened but we're not going to tell you'? It wasn't suicide. She didn't leave a note. Anyways, why jump? She was happy."

"Did they say anything about Teena?"

Des shook his head again. "Keeping an open mind."

"Did they know each other? I mean, online?"

Des shrugged. "Winnie had a lot of friends all over the world. Books meant a lot to her. That's why they asked her to come here, isn't it? I mean, sure, there was a contest. But there's always something at the back of it. It's the same if you win a vacation or anything, isn't it? Publicity. Cheap advertising. I don't mind. That's how the world works. Made my girl happy. You know?"

Emily suddenly remembered something. "Did she have a pronounced Southern accent?"

"No. We grew up around the same place. She talked the same as me."

"She hadn't been here before, had she? She must have been looking forward to coming here."

"Was she ever!"

Emily knew that was one of those American phrases that meant the opposite of what it ought to mean. "No-brainer" ought to mean stupid, but it didn't. "Lucked out" ought to mean out of luck, but it didn't. "Was she ever" ought to mean no, or at least express doubt of some kind, but it didn't. Fortunately, Emily watched her share of TV, so she knew Des was expressing enthusiastic agreement. If he had offered her a "re-up" on "the corners" she would have politely declined, though she'd have known what he meant by that as well, having watched all five seasons of *The Wire* on DVD.

"A tragedy like this reminds you people have good hearts. We only had the money for one airfare. That's why Win made the trip alone. The folks where we live, they got up a collection online to pay for my ticket to come here, and to pay for the service and the... the burial."

"That's nice. Americans always seem so community minded."

"There's people from all over the world who've contributed. Your organization, too. They donated a thousand bucks. That was a decent thing to do. I don't hold the romance writers responsible."

There was nothing she could say to Des by way of consolation for the loss of his wife. Instead, Emily stood companionably by his side, watching the tribute sites scroll by.

"Teena set these screens up. Pretty much the last thing she did before she died."

"Gee. That was nice of her. So it's a tribute to her as well. Kinda."

Page after page of book blogs scrolled by, crammed full of news and reviews. How did these people ever find time to read all those books, let alone write them up in such detail?

And then she saw one site that jarred, because it was out of keeping with all the rest. She bent to look. It was a little local news blog, full of parochial notices about village fetes, cricket matches, and plans to protest against a wind farm that would jeopardize a bird sanctuary. An anomaly! She got out her notebook and made a note.

"I'll be gone in the morning, early," Des said. "I've got to see about repatriating the body." He handed Emily a business card, misunderstanding the purpose of her note taking. "But if you want to ask me anything about Win, for a website or anything, you can send me an email. I'll be glad to talk. It's a way of remembering." Emily smiled a choked-up smile at Des and left him to his grief.

Emily was on her way down to the basement conference area to help Morgana set out the place cards for dinner when she bumped into Det. James.

"Rory, I wanted to talk to you!"

"Hey, Emily. Remembered something that might help the investigation?"

"No, I wanted to ask you something."

"You don't say?"

"You think the same person's responsible for Winnie's and Teena's deaths?"

"We're keeping an open mind."

"You don't think it's suicide, though? That doesn't make sense. That would be weird, wouldn't it?"

"Well, that's not how we'd present the facts to the coroner. But you're right. We're going through some...some documents we found on Teena. They give an indication of her state of mind."

"Documents? You mean like a note?"

"A notebook."

Emily blushed. "You shouldn't take too much notice of what people write in their notebooks."

"We have to take notice of everything. That's how an investigation works. Slow, methodical...Emily, have you ever heard of the One Star Club?"

"Does it exist, then?"

"That a yes or a no? Sounds like yes to me."

"It's a...well it's a long story. I don't think it's relevant."

"Oh, don't you? I'm already in trouble with my boss for cutting corners."

"The poison?"

"I can't tell you, Emily."

"Oh, *please* tell me. Please! I was right about the cyanide? At least admit it was possible."

"You want me to say it's possible you were right about a possible plan by one person to poison another?" He grinned. He was a naturally cheery person, despite the job he did.

"Yes!"

"Well it is possible. But I can't say it."

Emily grinned, too. First because maybe she was right about the cyanide, and she liked to be right as much as the next person. Second because all those possibles tumbling around where they didn't really belong made Emily think of wild, furry creatures—possums?—and reminded her of the unexpected sight she'd had recently of four fox cubs chasing each other in a playfight in her back garden. Third because he might have died from eating that chocolate, and he hadn't.

Emily and Morgana put out the place cards in the Montagu room according to the seating plan Morgana had made for dinner, except that they moved everybody on the right-hand side and everybody on the left-hand side up one place to close the gaps where Maggie and Teena should have been sitting. As they worked, Maria walked in between them, removing the specially-printed menu cards that had been placed on the tables, which were set up in a horseshoe shape, like a wedding breakfast, with Morgana to be placed at its head.

Emily and Morgana chatted about the menu—they were getting hungry—and, although they smiled and looked over at her when they spoke, to include her, Maria worked silently, even grimly, without looking up.

Emily picked up one of the menu cards Maria hadn't yet removed. "The goat cheese and roasted artichoke tart with beetroot chutney sounds nice," she said.

"Mmmm. You know you can get tubs of roasted artichoke hearts in Sainsbury's now? When I've had one of those days where I feel like absolute hell, sometimes I'll nip out and buy a tub, and then I'll sit in the kitchen and *gorge* myself on those delicious hearts. Oh! I sound like a novice satanic ritualist who has got mixed up about the specifics of the rites." Morgana giggled.

"Artichoke hearts are supposed to be good for your liver." Emily had a feeling Morgana might need to go on a detox tomorrow.

"I've tried to choose menu options that are light but filling. We don't want everyone getting too pissed. We've got health-conscious mains for those who care about such things. I hope they'll still be enough of a treat for those who don't. And, of course, I always want meat from an animal that has had a good life. Don't you?"

"I'm vegetarian."

"Oh, how tiresome for you." Morgana's sympathy was genuine. "Polly's the same. Kicked up a terrible fuss over a goose we tried to serve once for a RWGB Christmas dinner. Said why not go ahead and roast an angel and serve it up with sprouts and gravy if we wanted to be festive."

Emily laughed. She could imagine Polly saying it.

"All the food has been sourced from farms where the animals are allowed to wander at will, before being shot or strangled whatever it is that they do. Nik has been extremely helpful with the arrangements for dinner, fortunately."

Morgana had begun speaking self-consciously, which suggested to Emily that the subject of her conversation might be lurking near at hand. And there he was, hands wringing together in a way that indicated he was about to spill more bad news.

"The kitchens—"

"We're fortunate to be in such good hands, Nik. I saw a very nice review for the hotel restaurant in *Time Out* about two weeks ago."

"The kitchens have been shut for tonight. The police need to search the area after the, um, the unfortunate accident. They're questioning all the staff."

"I hope no one blames you. If someone's determined to climb over a fence on a roof, knowing it's dangerous, you can't be held accountable."

"I've got Health and Safety on my back, checking the fences upstairs, checking whether I, personally, might be criminally culpable—it carries a jail term. I'm afraid we can't allow your party to, uh, party on the roof."

"Oh, you poor thing! Never mind about us. Everything's gone wrong so far—nothing else bad can happen. That's the way we've got to deal with it. We shall look back on this at future conferences and no one will *ever* complain about anything again because everything will seem rosy in comparison."

"I admire your, uh…But I don't think you quite follow me. We can't serve a hot meal tonight. Our chef's preparing you a…well, it's a variation on our very popular Executive Brown-Bag Lunch. Of course, you're quite welcome to look elsewhere. I can have the concierge try and make reservations."

Even Morgana struggled to make the best of this news. But she did it. Eventually. "I don't think we can shift location. Where would forty of us even get in at this time on a Saturday night at this late notice?"

"There's that salsa place on Charing Cross Road. We've made inquiries, and they could do shared platters at a twenty percent discount. Your ladies and gentlemen would be very welcome to stay and dance afterward. It's popular with hen parties." Nik looked wretched. As well he might.

"A salsa bar on a Saturday night—that sounds like it might involve a little too much loud music and shouting. A brown-bag lunch sounds very…well it sounds very literary and hardworking, doesn't it? And American. One imagines T. S. Eliot having a brown-bag lunch."

"What *is* a brown-bag lunch?" asked Emily. Though she was vegetarian and she had developed a subtle palate, she couldn't imagine eating a brown paper bag, if that's what Nik was suggesting.

Nik explained, "It's a sort of picnic. Cold cuts. A slice of cake. A nectarine each, if we've got it. Chef said he thought he might have forty kiwi fruit. Of course, the wine tonight is on us."

"A picnic! Why, Virginia Woolf herself might have enjoyed it, then," Morgana said miserably, though she was trying to express delight. "And, thank you. We'll take you up on the free wine."

"I'll bring you in a glass each now of the white, so you can try it."

"*Would you!*" Morgana accidentally shouted. She was making too much effort not to sob to have any energy left over to regulate the volume at which she expressed her enthusiasm for wine.

As Nik went back through the service door to fetch the wine, Emily heard the incongruous sound of a voice singing mockingly: "Heigh-ho!"

Lex was one of the first dinner guests to arrive. Emily wondered where he'd been when Teena had been pushed off the roof. She was to be seated next to him, so perhaps she'd have a chance to ask him. Morgana had explained her decision to put Emily next to Lex by saying, "Lex does like the company of intelligent young women, he finds it very stimulating." She didn't say whether that was a good thing or a bad thing, and Emily felt that would rather depend on the crime he'd been accused of, though it shouldn't.

Lex had sat down in his place, and Morgana paused for a brief chat, leaning on the back of Dr. Muriel's empty chair, which was positioned on Lex's right side. Lex was in a generous mood.

"I could do a session at one of these things for you, Morgana. 'The Future of Publishing: New Ways of Working.'"

"Oh! Aren't you brilliant. I'll bear you in mind for a conference that *isn't* cursed—our next one, we hope. 'New Ways of Working'... You know, Lex, I've nearly finished my latest book, and while I was writing I kept thinking, there must be a better way of doing things. Ideally, I'd like to team up with someone."

"My client, Audrey Debenham—"

"Not Audrey. She writes too much like me. I'd want to write all the similes and pare down the prose. The other person would be responsible for the plot. Audrey'd be no good for that at all. Do you know what would be even better than teaming up?"

Morgana noticed she had finished her wine and interrupted herself while she looked around for a waitress to bring her a refill. Fortunately, she soon caught Maria's eye, and the soothing sound of wine sploshing into her glass signaled to her distressed mind that it was safe to resume the conversation. "Wouldn't it be great if you could just hire someone to outline for you, and then fill in the gaps, like those painting by numbers pictures that were popular in the 1970s? Do people do those anymore? Or do they just make videos of their children poking the cat in the eye and put it on YouTube? This millennium has more diverse outlets for the creatively minded, that's for sure."

"Well—" said Lex.

"Crafting's very popular with young women these days," said Emily. "Cross-stitch and knitting and quilting, but maybe with a slightly anarchic tone."

Apparently neither Lex nor Morgana was interested in crafting.

Morgana continued, "Even better than writing a book would be to find a way of transmitting the story directly into the reader's brain. It would dispense with the hours and *hours* of tedium sitting at the computer and getting it all down. I know that some writers say they'd like their books to be read as widely as possible, but I don't feel that way."

"You'll think differently once the latest book's done," Lex said. "This is just pre-delivery nerves."

"If people aren't going to like my books, I'd rather they left them alone and went and did something else. I'd be happy enough if just one person read my new book, so long as they liked it. Of course, that wouldn't be commercially viable—I do know that, Lex—unless I were to find a way to auction off the book for a million pounds." She brought up her hand to shield her mouth and murmured to Emily, "Though, privately, I don't mind admitting I'd probably accept ten thousand."

"You mustn't undersell yourself, Morgana," scolded Lex, who'd heard what she said very clearly.

"Forty thousand, then. Fifty! I'd leave the negotiations to you. Then I'd go off with this other person, and dream the book for them. It would be like having a love affair, except for the financial arrangements, and of course there would be no hard feelings when it was over, and no risk of disease. And no one-star reviews on Amazon, one hopes."

"For my Future of Publishing session I was thinking more along the lines of talking about ebooks. Twitter. Software for writing books, social media for marketing them. That type of thing."

"Oh yes! Yes. Marvelous. Where would writers be without agents? You do keep our feet on the ground."

Morgana swept off to take her place at the head of the table. Emily took out her notebooks and made a few notes.

"Are you a writer?" Lex asked, politely but resignedly. No doubt he thought Emily was going to pitch him her latest manuscript.

Emily put the notebook away. "No, no. I just wanted to write that down before I forgot it, because wouldn't that be a brilliant way to read a book? Having someone dreaming it directly into your head?"

"Not in our lifetime, alas. Though I must admit, I never thought I'd be able to hold a library in my hand. And yet they've found a way to do it." He held out his hand for a moment and shaped his fingers around an imaginary, orb-shaped e-reader, and he shook his head and smiled.

Emily asked him, "If they invented the technology to do the person-to-person book dreaming, and there was a risk involved, and they needed someone to test the prototype, would you volunteer?"

"Interesting. I've had a good long life. I've seen my children and my grandchildren grow up...No, I don't think I would. Would you, Emily?"

"I thought, when I was younger, that I'd like to be an explorer or an adventurer. But they're done with space exploration, aren't they? I can't see them going much further with that. I think they'll have to turn inward: explore the mind. So maybe I'd do it, if someone asked."

"Ah. And which book would you choose to have transmitted in such a way, direct from the author's mind into yours?"

"That's the thing. It would be a book that hadn't been dreamed of yet, wouldn't it? That's why it would be so exciting. That's why I'd do it."

Dr. Muriel arrived to take her place at Lex's right-hand side, with a cheery hello to Emily. Lex stood and drew out Dr. Muriel's chair for her, and ensured she was sitting comfortably. While he was doing that, Emily looked around the room as it filled up.

Cerys was to her left, and Zena was the other side of her. Polly and Archie were on the top table, a few places along on either side of Morgana. Among the other faces she recognized, Maggie was sitting opposite, on the other side of the horseshoe, next to a floppy-haired, youngish chap who was trying to chat to her. Emily couldn't hear what was being said, but she could see that Maggie was making a fuss about something. Emily made an *Are you all right?* face across the room. When it seemed she wasn't, Emily decided to go over there.

As the waiters and waitresses began to bring in the brown-bag meals—which were pretty much as described, being brown paper bags containing cold food—Morgana stood to welcome her guests. "Ladies and gentlemen, thank you for joining us at this gala dinner to celebrate this year's conference of the Romance Writers of Great Britain. For newcomers, I should explain that we are in no way affiliated to…" And on she went, much as she had at the start of the press conference, listing the names of all the august organizations that had no connection to the RWGB.

Emily ducked along the open end of the horseshoe and reached Maggie who explained the problem in a piercing whisper.

"I can't eat this."

"Are you allergic?"

"It's not that."

At the head of the table, Morgana was drawing her brief introduction to its conclusion. "And of course, Maggie Tambling—"

All eyes turned to the direction in which Morgana pointed her two upturned hands, like Judy Garland acknowledging the orchestra at Carnegie Hall.

Maggie's querulous whisper could be heard, quite distinctly. "What if it's poisoned?"

Morgana soldiered on. "Maggie Tambling, who is joining us for the first time after beating off fierce opposition to win our inaugural short fiction competition."

Morgana led the applause and then sat down and wordlessly raised her glass in a salute to the room, to signify that everyone should get on and eat, and drink. And then they could all go home.

"What makes you think it's poisoned?" Emily asked Maggie. "Was it something Teena said?"

Morgana had got up from her seat and was hurrying in their direction. "It's perfectly, perfectly OK, Maggie, I assure you."

"First Tallulah, then Teena. I don't want the next body in a bag to be me. Someone'll have to taste it before I eat it, won't they?"

"Darling, I think it's all over now. Their deaths were accidents. You're quite safe. There's no question of the food being poisoned."

It was unfortunate that just at that moment M. Loman burst in. "Poison!" he said. "Poison? Is this how you repay me?"

"Now," said Morgana, "Dear Monsieur Loman, I do think there might have been a mistake."

"I have never been so humiliated!"

Cerys whispered to Zena, "There speaks a man. Never had a smear test or a mammogram."

By now everyone was watching with the mixture of embarrassment and engagement familiar in small fringe theaters where the actors are just a little too close to the audience.

"First they break my heart. Is OK. It beats. I am still alive. Then they break my body. It hurts. Is OK. I am still alive. They cannot break my spirit. Cannot take my honor. I come here, to live among British people. I am safe, I think. But now, *you* try to take my livelihood. I will live. But I want to know why."

"Is this about the chocolates?"

"So you admit it!"

"No, no. Dear Monsieur Loman, please sit down and have a glass of wine. I wish I could do something…I wish I could do something kind for you, to show you that we mean you no harm."

"You wish to make reparation? A donation, then. To charity. Children of the Congo."

"I'll do it," Polly spoke up. "I'll be glad to do it. This is all my fault, anyway."

She picked up her handbag and took M. Loman by the arm. She led him outside to the lobby area where she had stuffed the gift bags with Emily, so she could make arrangements to send him a donation.

Maggie had watched all this without comment. As Polly came back in with the air of a deed well done, Maggie said to Morgana, "So there's no poison?"

"Absolutely not. No."

Maggie pushed her brown-bag executive lunch toward Morgana. "You won't mind tasting this for me, then?"

Morgana did mind, obviously. But she acquiesced. And so Maggie picked up her handbag and walked to the head of the table. Room was made, and a chair was found, so she could sit next to Morgana. Morgana then proceeded to take up her knife and fork and cut mouselike bites out of the various items that had been supplied to Maggie in the brown bag, putting them in her mouth, chewing thoroughly and then swallowing them under Maggie's direction, before Maggie consented to eat them. Morgana also tasted the wine before it was served. With her jaunty pink fez and tragicomic expression, Morgana made a passably good jester and chief food taster to Maggie's intransigent monarch. When Morgana went out to the front of the hotel to stand by the steps and smoke, Maggie watched impatiently for her return.

At some point, before she got too drunk, Morgana rose to make a simple, moving tribute to Winnie. "Let us not forget the power of words to live on after we die, and move those who read them…"

As she spoke, Cerys leaned in to whisper to Zena, "They're not going to leave up her website, now she's gone? Surely they'll take down her reviews?"

"Immortality, innit, babes? You want them to shred your books after you've gone?"

"No, I'd hope sales would soar."

"There you are, then. Her website will have more visitors than ever."

Cerys sighed. "I suppose I'll just have to get on and write the next book, then."

At the head of the table, Morgana concluded by saying, "Winnie's talent was not for writing fiction, much as we must admire her for trying. Winnie's talent came when she donned the mask as Tallulah, and she wrote about her appreciation for other people's talent for writing fiction. She was witty, she was funny, she was truthful. We need people who have her talent for appreciating books. Not many can do it. She found her true talent before she died. Not many can say that. She was appreciated. She achieved something. What she achieved will endure. To Winnie!"

As the people around the room raised their glasses in a toast, Emily instinctively looked toward the door. By rights, Des should have been standing there with tears in his eyes, having slipped in unannounced to hear this moving tribute. But this wasn't a British romcom film. Des wasn't standing by the door, he was upstairs in his room grieving.

After that the evening was a success because everyone who was involved in publishing got very, very drunk and gossiped about other people in the publishing industry. These were activities that revived memories of a halcyon past and seemed to cheer everyone up—even those who didn't have much faith in the future of publishing. And then, to cap it all, at about ten o'clock Polly got a call from her agent in New York, which of course is five hours behind London in temporal terms, and twenty years ahead in lots of other ways. But no one was considering the other ways tonight.

Morgana rose from her seat and dinged her glass. "We've just had some wonderful news. Wonderful! Polly Penham has been nominated for a Lifetime Achievement Award by the Romance Authors of America."

"RAA!" a few people said, in tiger growls of appreciation.

"Lifetime achievement?" Emily overheard Zena saying to Cerys. "She's only thirty-three!"

Cerys shuddered. "I wouldn't want to be presented with a lifetime achievement award, even at my age, a grandmother with nearly thirty books to my name. Bad luck, see? I mean, where do you go after that? It's all over, isn't it?"

"Yeah…Hadn't thought of it that way. You think it's a warning? The universe is trying to tell Polly something?"

"No I don't! I'm an agnostic Presbyterian. Besides, any more bad news and I won't need to dye my hair this color. I'll wake up tomorrow and my roots'll have turned platinum blonde overnight."

"No more expensive visits from the hairdresser. If it happens, it'll be the first time in your life that coming up to London ever saved you money, Cerys."

The two women laughed the special laugh some women reserve for acknowledging extravagance, especially as it relates to overspending on clothes or shoes. But as events unfolded that night, Emily—also an agnostic—had cause to wonder whether the universe might, after all, be trying to communicate some sort of warning. To all of them.

CHAPTER FIFTEEN
THE HERO

The gala dinner ended with everyone in good spirits. Some of the younger members of the RWGB and their guests made plans to go on to a club in Soho to drink overpriced drinks and mingle with television presenters, actors and former pop stars. Others went home. Those who remained, including most of the committee, Emily, Dr. Muriel and Maggie, professed themselves too tired to do anything but fall into bed to sleep, in preparation for the long day ahead.

Lex kissed Morgana goodbye as he hailed a taxi to take him home. "What a magnificent evening. You know I'd go to the ends of the earth to attend one of your marvelous conferences."

Morgana said, "I don't believe a word of it. You old fraud!" And then both she and Lex looked terribly embarrassed, and Emily thought she might have an idea of the crime Lex had once been accused of.

There was lots of kissing on both cheeks, and hugging and laughter, and then the hotel went quiet. There was the muffled sound, now and again, of people laughing too loudly in the street outside as they walked home or waited to get a night bus. The thick walls of the hotel kept out most of the noise, including the traffic sounds. As she fell asleep, Emily heard the occasional cry of an urban fox, which sounds like the desperate call of a man being stabbed. She dreamed of four foxes playfighting in her garden in South London.

The toast's burning! thought Emily. *I've got to get up before the smoke alarm goes off.*

And then the alarm went off. And then she thought, *I'm not making toast.*

She was awake, and outside it was pandemonium. Again.

"Fire!" someone called. "Fire! Come on, now. Everybody out. Walk, don't run."

Knuckles rapped at her door, flung it open and moved on. *Don't mind me!* thought Emily. Fortunately, she was wearing cream-colored pajamas with blue bunnies on them. When choosing night-wear to take with her on trips away from home, Emily had noticed that most manufacturers seemed to think women of her age were either sex-starved sluts or oversize toddlers who craved a return to the nursery. Though she was aware she looked ridiculous in her bunnies, she was glad at least that her natural prudishness had saved her the embarrassment of running about Bloomsbury in something flimsy that showed her nipples.

Further down the corridor Emily heard the knocking, the doors being flung open, and the almost robotically calm repetition of the words, "Everybody out. Walk, don't run."

There was the shrill, persistent sound of a fire alarm and, underneath that, the sound of people running or walking from their rooms, doors slamming. Emily looked at the digital display on the alarm clock provided by the hotel at the side of her bed. It was 3:13.

Outside it was dark.

Inside there was the smell of smoke.

Outside, the darkness was now punctuated by flashing blue lights and the terse shouts of trained men and women doing something useful.

Inside, Emily put on her shoes and grabbed her handbag and notebook.

Outside, guests were gathering in Russell Square at the designated evacuation point.

Emily walked out of her room, walked down the emergency stairs, walked out of the hotel.

As she crossed the street and walked toward the square, she could see other guests waiting calmly in their nightclothes, clutching whatever was of most value to them—handbags, notebooks (there being a lot of writers in residence), laptop computers, armfuls of clothes. Most were wearing the pale-blue, cotton bathrobes provided by the hotel. Some guests stood in small groups without possessions. Their stoic expressions, and the bathrobes, gave the impression that they were invalids from a sanatorium who had been bidden to go into the square to get some fresh air for their health.

Once she was at the assembly point, Emily turned and looked at the hotel, expecting to see it half up in flames with the roof crumbling in. But it was standing imperturbably, as it had done for more than a century. There were only a few puffs of smoke coming from a couple of second floor windows. These were already being treated with water by the firefighters from the fire engine underneath the windows. A second engine drew up and parked next to it, but perhaps it wouldn't be needed. An ambulance was parked in front of the hotel on the other side. Emily certainly hoped that that wouldn't be needed.

Then one of the windows on the second floor was smashed open and a distraught man called from inside, "Sookie! Sheena? Sheena, where are ye, hen?"

A firefighter used a loud-hailer to call up to him: "Sir, would you please evacuate the building."

"Emily, m'dear. Glad to see you're safe." Emily turned to see Dr. Muriel in a sensible pair of navy pajamas and a quilted, maroon dressing gown, carrying a large bar of fruit and nut chocolate and her silver-topped cane. "Is that Archie?"

They heard the man's voice again. It was almost a shriek. "Sheena!"

"You think I should go back in for him?"

"I'd say that rather exceeds the scope of your terms of employment."

"I know. But—"

"I don't think he's in danger. He woke from a nightmare, I expect. He'll come down presently." She removed the wrapper from her bar of chocolate and broke it into pieces, apportioning four squares each to whoever nearby put their hand out for it. Emily had some and it was very nice, though she could have done with a cup of tea to wash it down.

Polly strolled up. She was wearing dark-blue, cotton pajamas and a mannish, sensible, dark-blue robe tied tight at the waist. She held a packet of cheddar-cheese-flavored biscuits, a bottle of opened red wine, and two of the stubby porcelain cups that were provided in the guest bathrooms by the hotel for the storage of toothbrushes. "This is like boarding school. All it lacks is a bottle of rum and some playing cards. And some naughty sixth-form boys."

Emily caught sight of Des standing alone to one side of the square. If he'd had a flaming torch in his hand, she wouldn't have blamed him. But he wasn't responsible for the fire. His fists clenched and unclenched at nothing, and he looked down at the ground almost oblivious to what was going on around him. He didn't look as though he wanted company, and Emily didn't go over and offer it.

"Polly," said Emily, "Des said someone from the RWGB contributed a thousand dollars to Winnie's online fund."

"You think it looks like blood money? I wanted to provide some practical help on behalf of all of us. Don't worry, I can afford it." She grinned. "Just don't tell Zena. She'll think I'm being flash."

The crowd in the square murmured appreciatively as two fire-fighters appeared at the entrance to the hotel with a large black woman on a stretcher and carried her toward the ambulance. The woman appeared to be conscious. The purple-polished fingertips of one hand gripped the oxygen mask that had been strapped to her head. It was Zena.

"Thank Christ for that! She looks all right, doesn't she? Bit of smoke inhalation, maybe? Least she's not burned to a crisp." Cerys had joined them, in a silk kimono and fluffy, red, high-heeled mules, all her diamond rings on her fingers. Either she slept in them or she'd had the good sense not to leave them behind on the dressing table in an unlocked room. She was carrying three shopping bags of clothes and smoking a cigarette. "Doesn't seem right to be chuffing on this, under the circumstances," she admitted with a shrug. But she didn't put the cigarette out. "Oh my...look at that!"

Another murmur from the crowd. Standing at the entrance to the hotel, framed for a moment by the light behind him in an almost parodic silhouette of a hero, was a slender man in white silk pajama bottoms and bare feet, naked from the waist up. Slung across his shoulders was the even more slender figure of a woman in a smart jacket and skirt.

"Can't see who it is," Dr. Muriel said. "Is it a ninja, Emily?"

His coppery-red hair hung damply over one eye, and as he be-gan to move toward them and into the light of the street lamps outside the hotel, they saw his face and chest were streaked with sooty dirt. It was Archie.

Cerys provided a commentary. "Archie, carrying a woman. She seems to be alive, thanks be. Is that Sheena, you think? He's found his Sheena? Aww. Bless him. I didn't realize he'd brought anyone with him this weekend. Who'd have thought? Oh, look out! He's coming this way."

In fact, Archie had not found Sheena. Sheena was the name of his long-dead sister and, though he often searched for her in his dreams and his nightmares, he would never find her. Nor his sister Sookie, either. The woman whose body was slung across his shoulders was Miss Wendy Chen, who had been on night duty on the hotel's Reception desk and hadn't needed rescuing. She was thoroughly drilled in evacuation techniques and had only recently completed all necessary components of the Hotel Evac Refresher Course, a prerequisite for joining this hotel from the one where she had recently been posted in Singapore.

As she had completed the last checks on the rooms on the second floor this evening, Wendy was astonished to find herself grabbed out of the smoky darkness and carried down two flights of stairs. She had wriggled and slapped Archie on his bare shoulders, furious at the effrontery. She was aware that some Western men subscribed to the myth that Asian women were docile or acquiescent. She didn't intend to start her career in this country being *plundered* by a Scottish pirate. But then he'd staggered about with her on his shoulders bellowing "Sookie! Sookie! Where are ye, hen?" and she'd come to understand that he was searching for lost poultry and was therefore insane, and she'd stopped struggling, and stopped worrying about antifeminist Western myths, and started to calculate whether it made better sense financially to sue the hotel management for compensation for kidnap, or simply to demand a much more senior job when this crisis was over. If the former, then she needed to act hysterical and injured. If the latter, then she should remain calm, and take control of the situation as soon as she could.

Fortunately for Archie, she decided on the latter course. After he set her down on the grass in Russell Square, he began shouting for Sookie again.

"He's going back in," someone said admiringly—a fan of American disaster films, perhaps.

The crowd in Russell Square weren't the only ones watching his antics. A voice came over the loud-hailer again. "Sir! Sir, please do *not* endanger yourself. Do *not* attempt to regain entry to the premises until someone from the London Fire Brigade has given the all clear."

"Sookie! Ahm coming tae get ye."

Wendy Chen composed herself. She drew back her left elbow and floored Archie with a magnificent left hook. "Not a good idea to endanger yourself for a chicken," she said. She went over to talk to the most senior London Fire Brigade officer on duty to see what should be done next.

As she left, several women in their nightdresses rushed forward from the crowd to tend to Archie's fallen body. With his handsome, sensitive, high-cheekboned face, his sorrowful eyes fluttering open toward consciousness, he looked like a shell-shocked, poetry-writing infantry officer from World War I.

"What was Archie in prison for, anyone remember?" asked Cerys. "It wasn't arson, was it?"

CHAPTER SIXTEEN
MELTED BARBIE

The ambulance set off for the hospital, Zena aboard, blue lights flashing, sirens silent out of respect for those sleeping in this mainly residential area. Morgana now came out to the square to check up on the RWGB members that she could pick out in the crowd.

Across the street Emily saw Det. James, obviously not long out of bed himself, though fully dressed. He got out of an unmarked squad car and went up the steps into the hotel. He was followed by uniformed officers who arrived in another car.

"What's the news, M?" asked Cerys as Morgana reached her side. "Can we go back in?"

"What a ghastly night. Yes, they said we can make our way back in. All the rooms can be occupied, except Zena's. They may keep her overnight in the hospital for observation. But if not, the hotel will find her another room. They're prepared to move anyone else who asks, particularly if they're on the second floor. Just speak to Wendy Chen at Reception."

Emily said, "What happened, has anyone told you?"

"The fire started in Zena's room, that's all I know. Seems she unscrewed the smoke detector on the ceiling. Probably wanted to smoke in her room. You have to be so *careful* about that sort of thing. You know, someone once tried to teach me a technique for smoking in an airplane toilet that involves flushing the loo and simultaneously exhaling, but if you don't time it right—well, either you get sucked half-out of the plane or you set off the alarms. Either way it's an ignominious way to draw attention to yourself. Not that I've tried it. I've only thought about it. I wish Zena had only thought about doing this."

Dr. Muriel said, "I vote we go back in and try and get some sleep. I don't want anyone missing my Ethics in Literature session first thing. On that note, can we meet beforehand, Emily? Over breakfast? Nine o'clock? I'd like to discuss a few ideas with you."

It was nearly five o'clock now. Dawn was opening up the gray tin can of the London skyline, and the birds in the trees were starting to sing. Quite loudly.

"Listen to that! I could gladly shoot the lot of them," said Cerys.

"Imagine a world without birds," said Polly. "It doesn't bear thinking about. Mao tried it, and when the birds dropped out of the sky with exhaustion and a plague of locusts came, the people were soon sorry." She walked quickly toward the hotel empty-handed, leaving the remnants of her boarding-school-style midnight feast discarded at the foot of a tree in the square.

"Well, that's me told!" said Cerys.

Emily was so tired she thought that if she were a bird, she'd drop like a stone from the sky. She said to Dr. Muriel, "Shall we say nine thirty?"

Dr. Muriel nodded and rushed ahead. No doubt she could sleep anywhere. She was an intrepid traveler who had told Emily she was happy enough with third-class accommodation on foreign trains. Emily imagined her friend propping herself into a corner, folding her arms and sleeping with the untroubled dreams of someone who thought very deeply about things when she was awake.

Emily hung back a little to keep pace with Morgana. She wanted to ask her a question. They went into the hotel and began to climb the stairs.

"Is it true that Archie's been in prison?"

"Hmm? Yes. That's where I met him. My creative writing program Write Back Where You Belong. I teach some of the classes. Lex is a patron. Good night, Emily, and thanks for everything. You'll be glad to get back to the nine-to-five after this, won't you?"

Morgana darted off into the corridor on the first floor where her bedroom was located. Emily tramped up to the second floor. She was fit, but she wasn't used to climbing stairs. She thought she might have a rest. And what better way to rest than to loiter here on the second floor for a bit, and then have a quick look at Zena's burned-out room? Though she shouldn't have been on the second floor, Emily didn't attract attention. There were plenty of people coming and going, fetching washbags and a few clothes for the next day from their smoke-damaged rooms: most of the guests who had been staying on the second floor had been allocated rooms on other floors.

As she was officially helping Morgana at the conference, Emily had seen a list with all the RWGB guests' room numbers. She knew Zena's room was along the end here, something like 236 or 238—though she didn't really need to know the number. All she had to do was follow the smoke.

The door to Zena's room was open and Emily peeped in. She saw the charred, damp remains of many purple fashion accessories, including a trilby hat which she had never seen Zena wearing. In the corner of the room, on the dressing table, was the most blackened item. It was shaped like a miniature playhouse or a diorama. At first Emily could only think that it was some kind of apparatus that Zena used to develop her stories, though the objects inside it seemed like strange choices if they were to represent characters in a play. There was a very small glazed pot and a small silver bell, of the kind that a very polite, bedridden invalid might ring to summon help from a family member. In the middle of this diorama was something melted that Emily recognized by its nylon, yellow hair as the remains of Barbie doll. A few scraps of the doll's clothes were now fused to her misshapen body: she had once been dressed in pink.

Emily looked at the bell and the Barbie doll, and she suddenly knew what this "diorama" must be. It was Zena's altar. If the Barbie doll represented who she thought it represented, then somewhere in this room...Yes, over there! A Topshop bag. And, inside it, a little pink cardigan with a piece cut out of it, the size roughly suitable to be used to fashion a crude costume for a doll.

She heard Det. Rory James's voice, in earnest discussion with other voices she didn't recognize, heading in her direction, and she stuffed the ruined cardigan back in the bag. As the voices drew nearer, she found it easier to make out the words. One of Det. James's colleagues was saying "...blueprint for murder. Stabbing. Arson. Dogs attacking...Notebook...Seems to make the case for a propensity to violence against women..."

She darted out of Zena's room and walked back along the corridor, as nonchalantly as possible. Rory nodded at her in greeting but continued his conversation with his two colleagues without breaking his stride. The three of them stopped when they reached Zena's room, and one of the uniformed officers got out some blue-and-white tape, and began to seal off the area.

As Emily continued walking along the corridor toward the stairs, Dr. Muriel poked her head out of her room.

"Emily!"

"Isn't it too smoky for you here? I could ask the hotel to find you another room."

"That's fine, m'dear. Reminds me of Tibet." Dr. Muriel jerked her head in the direction of Zena's room. "Been having a look? Got everything you need for tomorrow, I hope?"

"What's happening tomorrow?"

"Ah. I thought you'd realized when I asked if we could move my session to kick off the conference. Tomorrow's the denouement."

CHAPTER SEVENTEEN
THE DENOUEMENT

Emily would have said she'd hardly slept at all. But she'd had crazy, smoke-filled dreams, with Archie shouting and breaking out of prison with Lex, and policemen in uniform dropping dead after eating poisoned artichoke hearts, and Morgana and Polly holding hands and jumping off the roof and calling, "It's OK, Emily. We can fly. Come and join us."

It's said that a good night's sleep is a wonderful way to put your thoughts in order. If true, then there was no surer indication that Emily hadn't had a good night's sleep. She still had no clear idea about what had happened to Winnie and Teena. Perhaps Dr. Muriel knew what she was doing and they could expect a confession from someone that morning, and Emily wouldn't have to worry about making sense of things.

She went into the Brunswick room to find that dozens of people had washed in again for the vigil, their presence and absence seeming almost tidal. The pile of cellophane-wrapped flowers was a little higher than yesterday, and the sweet rotting-compost smell that came from the lower layers was more noticeable. Several toy cats had also been left under the table, in acknowledgment of Winnie's love for her pet. Apparently stuffed representations of Maine coon cats were hard to find in London, because people had brought in black-and-white cats, ginger cats, pink cats. The ginger cats were the most popular. Small ginger cats were on special offer in WHSmith, and there were two branches of the shop in nearby King's Cross station.

Frazer the bookseller was setting up his stall again, with the cheeriness of someone who expects to make a good few sales. Polly's pile of books had a beautifully written notice next to it: *Nominated for a RAA Lifetime Achievement Award.* Polly was at the table, in a pale pink trouser suit, hair tied back neatly, pen in hand, signing books. She looked up at Emily and smiled, and rubbed her wrist ruefully (she had a lot of copies to sign) and then got back to work.

Emily went to the hotel dining room to meet Dr. Muriel for breakfast. The kitchen was functioning again—presumably the police had completed their search—and there were a lot of tired, grumpy, hungover people in the hotel dining room eating the full English breakfast: bacon, sausage, eggs, tomatoes, mushrooms and toast.

Emily opened her notebook and studied it while she was waiting for her vegetarian option of wild woodland mushrooms and vegetarian sausages with toasted sunflower bread to arrive.

"Do you know who's responsible for these women's deaths, Dr. Muriel?"

"Certainly not. That's your department. It's all in your notebook." Dr. Muriel tapped it for emphasis. "You are a young woman who is full of ideas, Emily Castles. Now comes the time to put them to the test."

"I do have ideas. Also wild theories, prejudices and unfounded suspicions. Also, in some areas, no ideas at all."

As if he'd been summoned to back this up, Det. James wandered past and pulled up a chair. He looked exhausted. Dr. Muriel poured him some orange juice from a jug on the table. "Don't you ever stop working, Rory?"

"Doesn't look like it," he said amiably. "What about you?"

Dr. Muriel laughed as though she'd been caught out. "Observing, always observing. And cogitating. Or daydreaming, as my mother used to call it. She would not have approved if she'd known I get paid to do it. Any news, dear boy?"

"Not exactly."

"Not exactly." Dr. Muriel seemed satisfied with this. She munched on a piece of eggy toast.

"My boss is saying he should have brought in a more senior officer, right from the start."

"That's the sort of thing bosses say, though, isn't it? I'm always catching hell from mine. You must be glad, Emily, that you don't have a boss that you're permanently answerable to. You do have them, of course. But you can chop and change. There must be a feeling of freedom in that."

Emily's vegetarian breakfast arrived, and she gloomily did her best to enjoy the feeling of freedom that came with knowing she'd be out of a job again tomorrow.

Nik Kovacevic approached the table. "Everything all right, ladies? Please accept the hotel's apologies for last night's events. There were circumstances, as I'm sure you realize, that were beyond our control."

"Yes," said Dr. Muriel. "Emily has a theory about it."

Rory James rolled his eyes good-humoredly and drained his orange juice.

Nik said, "We run a very popular murder mystery evening here at the hotel. If you like 'investigating,' Emily, you should think about booking for that."

Rory James laughed and stood up to leave.

Dr. Muriel laughed, too. "I think we need to get things wrapped up soon, don't you? There might be other lives at stake. If you gentlemen aren't too busy, perhaps you'd be kind enough to join my session at the conference at ten o'clock."

They both looked startled. Det. James said, "Why, what's happening?"

"Emily's going to tell you whodunit."

A little bit of toasted sunflower bread went down the wrong way, and Emily started to choke. Rory James thumped her on the back. Emily recovered enough to wash down the toast with a reviving cup of tea. She reminded herself that if things went horribly wrong, she'd never have to see any of these people again.

Dr. Muriel heaved herself to her feet. "All set?"

"I need to spend a few minutes in the room where they're holding the vigil."

"Ha! Quiet contemplation among the shabby cats and the wilting flowers? Or are you fossicking for clues? No! Don't tell me. I'll wait for the denouement. See you downstairs."

In the Montagu room, as the basement conference space was officially known, Morgana was testing that the projector was working, by turning it on, then off, then on again. She was wearing a tartan waistcoat and a Tam o' Shanter—a tartan bonnet with a red pom-pom on the crown. She seemed jittery. Maria was putting out the last of forty pads and pencils at intervals along the horseshoe-shaped tables.

"I wonder if I should have asked for the tables to be set up cabaret style?" mused Morgana, as if to deliberately provoke Maria, who took no notice. "I suppose it's too late now. Are you all set for this morning, Emily? Muriel's cooking up something, isn't she? But she won't tell me what it is."

Emily felt that Dr. Muriel was treating her like the subject of one of those science experiments at school, where you're invited to touch a Van de Graaff generator and your hair stands up on end without you doing anything clever at all. But she also felt strangely…confident. All the information was there in her head. She just had to spool it out carefully, in the right order.

She decided she was up to the challenge. Why not? After five o'clock today she was finished, anyway. They couldn't very well sack her if she got it all wrong.

Once everyone had filed in, Morgana stood to open the conference officially. There were surprisingly few gaps around the table considering what a late night everyone had had. All the members of the organizing committee were there, including Zena and Archie. Whereas there had been a table plan for dinner last night, seats at the conference this morning were unallocated. Emily noticed that Archie had a pretty brunette woman sitting to his left, and a pretty brunette woman sitting to his right, both looking at him expectantly, as if it wouldn't be the end of the world if there was a fire and Archie had to strip his shirt off to rescue them.

There were faces Emily recognized from last night, though she didn't know their names. The thing about working on short-term, temporary contracts like this was that you got to know some people very, very well, and others…others you didn't get to know and would never see again. They were like churchyard statues. No doubt they had lived rich and interesting lives. But to strangers passing quickly by, they were interchangeable gray figures, their features blurry and unmemorable. And Emily was passing by very quickly.

"I have learned something this weekend," said Morgana by way of introduction to the day's sessions. "Some of us are writers, some of us are readers, some of us are reviewers. Most of us only really have one talent, and we should be thankful for it and exploit it. We have seen the death of two talented women. They weren't much good as writers of fiction. I'm sorry. It's true. I brought them here under false pretenses, and I shouldn't have done it. I valued them for one talent—as bloggers—and instead of celebrating that, I brought them here and feted them as writers of fiction. And I hope to goodness, I really do, that my chicanery didn't result in either of their deaths.

"We will have an opportunity to consider that, perhaps, during Muriel's session on ethics, which will start us off this morning. Then after the break, we have Zena with 'What am I? A Piece of Wood?'—a look at the depiction of people of color in literature. Then lunch. Would you all please take time to pop in to the Brunswick room and sign copies of your books for anyone who has bought them? Then after lunch we've Cerys with 'Don't Ask Me! I'm Only a Woman.' Then I'll finish up with 'Whither the Novel,' at the end of which we'll have a chance to talk about next year's conference, and what we might do differently.

"Without further ado, I'll hand you over to Dr. Muriel Crowther."

Rather than walk to the front, Dr. Muriel remained where she sat, and addressed the room. "What must be done," she asked, "when we're dealing with real life people in our stories? Do we have a greater obligation to them than to the creatures of our imagination, much as we love them?"

If any of the authors present balked at the use of "we" they didn't show it. Dr. Muriel had published twelve books, including two biographies of famous psychiatrists and two of famous Victorian charlatans (she was fond of inviting her audiences to comment on whether or not she should simply say she had written the biographies of four charlatans), so although she didn't generate stories in the same way as the romance writers in the room, she knew what she was talking about.

Archie spoke up from across the room. "I think we have to honor them."

"Yes indeed. You see, something very strange has happened this weekend. A story has been created before our eyes, and it has involved real people, and some of them have got hurt. It hurt so much, they're dead."

Dr. Muriel spoke softly. Everyone leaned forward, intrigued to hear what she would say next.

She said something that surprised everyone who wasn't expecting it: "So now I'm going to turn you over to Emily Castles, a very bright young woman whom all of you have met. And she's going to explain what happened, and how, and why. Detective James, can you confirm that your men are standing by at the other side of the doors, please?"

Everyone looked round at Det. James, standing in front of the door with Nik Kovacevic, who looked as though he might faint. Det. James nodded.

"Very well. Let's begin."

Emily also remained in her seat. She had no need to walk up to the front and switch on the projector—it wasn't as if she'd prepared any slides. She took out her notebook and laid it on the table in front of her. Her stomach turned over and over, presumably with nerves, though perhaps she shouldn't have eaten those vegetarian sausages.

"I can't claim to know all the answers. Anything that struck me as strange over the last twenty-four hours, I wrote it down. Some of it related to the story—"

"Why call it a story? Isn't it usually called a 'case'?" one of the churchyard statues called.

"Calling it a 'case' sounds a bit pompous," admitted Emily.

Cerys defended her. "Let her call it a story if she wants to call it a story."

"Some of what I'd written down relates to the story, and some of it relates to me. And I spent ages trying to disentangle the two before I realized I was in this story, too."

"Too right, babes. Everything's connected. That's the way the universe works. She's got a wise head on them shoulders!" Zena's voice was slightly hoarse because of the smoke she'd inhaled before being hauled out of her room the night before.

"And then—Dr. Muriel's right—I realized someone was writing this story for us, and turning the pages, and telling us what we should see. There were too many clues. Way, way too many. That's because there was more than one story. There was the murder story, and all our personal stories mixed up with it, and other stories as well. And someone had been planting superfluous clues, which didn't help. But I'll get to that. Two things seemed to be important, though at first I couldn't see why. In fact, I wondered if they had nothing to do with Winnie's and Teena's deaths and they only were bothering me because…well, because they always bother me. The first was smoking. How many people smoke, here?"

Just under half the people in the room raised their hands, including Zena, Cerys and Morgana.

"The other one was litter."

"Ha!" Dr. Muriel looked around the room, nodding sagely at anyone who would meet her eye.

"But the big question seemed to be, why was Winnie invited here? If her death wasn't a random attack, had she been *invited here to die?*"

"Ooh," said most of the people in the room, though there were also some "hmms."

"I think, if you don't mind, I'll start at the end and work backward."

"Who are you? Martin Amis?" This from another of the gray, blurry faces whose name Emily didn't know and would never probably know. She ignored him.

"First of all, the fire. It could have been an attempt to destroy evidence, couldn't it? It could have been an attempt to intimidate witnesses, or even kill someone in their sleep. The two main players in the story of the fire were Zena and Archie. It started in Zena's room, and the person who was most affected by the fire—or seemed most affected by it—was Archie. Both are members of the organizing committee who voted to bring Winnie here. Winnie, of course, ran a popular blog under the name Tallulah."

"Tallulah's Treasures? Well I never! Did everyone else know?" Cerys looked around. Approximately half the people in the room nodded. The other half stared blankly. "Where've I been, then? Stuck under a rock? Well, blow me down." She wasn't a very good actress. No one believed her.

"I think you said, didn't you Cerys, that you'd like to get your hands on Tallulah and teach her a lesson, because she'd written you a nasty review?"

"I'd have liked to have words, if that's what you mean. Wouldn't we all?"

There were general sounds of demurral from around the room, as if to suggest that nobody present had ever received a poor review, and if they had, they wouldn't be so silly as to get upset by it.

Only Polly spoke up for her. "I think we all get cross when we see someone has written something unkind about us. Don't these people realize we have families and friends who might read what they have written? Don't they realize that we ourselves have feelings? It doesn't mean we'd kill someone over it."

"What about you, Zena? There was a melted doll on the altar in your room last night. It is an altar, isn't it?"

182

"My books are smoking hot, babes. But I've never set fire to a doll on an altar. Anyone ever had a bad review from a doll? Didn't think so! No one has. Certainly not Zena."

"You weren't trying to bring harm to someone?"

"Nope."

"The doll was dressed in pink, to represent Polly."

"Ooh!" Everyone in the room turned to look at Polly. Polly remained absolutely still and quiet. Her face was inscrutable.

"You'd disconnected the smoke alarm in your room, hadn't you?"

"Yeah, well. Gotta put my hand up to that. Didn't want to go outside on them chilly steps to have a puff. That's not a crime, is it?"

From the back of the room, Nik Kovacevik piped up, "Actually—"

Emily ignored him and addressed Zena. "You heard the news that Polly had been nominated for a Lifetime Achievement Award and you...you put a likeness of her on the altar to wish her luck after dinner last night." Emily suspected that Zena might not have been wishing luck to Polly. But Zena took her cue, gratefully.

"Yeah. Yeah. That's it, babes. Even someone as successful as Polly, she can do with a little Zena luck."

"Mmmmm," said the people in the room. Everyone looked at Polly. Polly smiled graciously.

"You lit your incense and made your wish, and when you went to sleep something on the altar caught fire—maybe the hot tip of the incense touched part of the doll's clothes. Whatever it was, it didn't trigger the alarm because you'd dismantled it. And you were oblivious until you were dragged out of bed by the firefighters."

Zena chuckled. "I was having me some sexy dreams."

"So the fire was a separate story that got mixed up with the murder story. It wasn't relevant at all."

"What about Archie?" asked the brunette sitting to his left.

"Ach. I was having me some nightmares."

Emily looked up at Det. James as she said, "Sometimes it helps to write them down, doesn't it? It doesn't mean anything."

Rory James grinned at her in a way that plainly said: *Yeah! Thanks for the hint. Tell me something I don't know.*

"What was peculiar about this...*case* was that Winnie's body was moved after her death. We all agree that she fell from the roof terrace, don't we? Or was pushed?"

Det. James said, "Mrs. Kraster was pushed. She offered no resistance, but she was pushed."

"Aha!" said Dr. Muriel.

"Same thing with Teena Durani."

Emily was now feeling confident enough to play to the room a little. "But why didn't they offer any resistance?"

"Hypnotism?" suggested Morgana. "Some sort of weird secret society cult thing?"

"How about hairspray?" countered Emily.

"Ahhh!" said all the women in the room who had ever attended a self-defense class.

"A face full of that would be enough to distract the victim. Temporarily blinded, one shove and she'd topple over the fence to her death. Then it would have needed two strong people to move her body to the housing estate next to the hotel. Two women, maybe. Two members of the organizing committee who'd lured Winnie here to her death."

"Oh, Emily!" said Morgana in a very, very hurt voice. "Darling, no. Which of us would do such a thing?"

"Cerys?"

"Well I never!" said Cerys. "The worm turns."

"A quick burst of hairspray and a shove, and Winnie and her review site are silenced for good. And then Cerys and her friend Zena move the body."

"Ach!" Archie was furious. "Here we go. Blame the black woman in the room."

Emily was still playing to the room. "But why?"

"Because society's inherently racist and you can't help yourself, hen."

"No, I meant why would they move the body. It doesn't make any sense. So maybe it's not Cerys and Zena. Maybe it's not the organizing committee who moved the body. Maybe it's someone at the hotel."

Emily continued, her eyes on Nik Kovacevic, "Two strong men who know the layout of the hotel, who know how to temporarily dismantle the CCTV, who want to protect the reputation of the hotel. A porter, maybe. And a...a manager."

There was a scraping sound as Nik drew back a chair and sat down. He seemed to need to take the weight off his legs before they gave in under him.

"But why would they kill a guest at the hotel?" Emily continued, "It didn't seem like it would be very good for business."

"The One Star Club!" said Cerys. "Got to be."

"The One Star Club," said Emily, for the benefit of the people in the room who hadn't been privy to Dr. Muriel's fabrication, "is supposed to be an international club. Its members undertake to leave one star reviews for books, goods and services online."

There were lots of "Ohhhhs!" Everyone—they were all authors in the room, except for Rory, Nik, Maria and Maggie—liked the idea of a conspiracy. It fitted with the deep-seated belief they all had that no genuine readers of their books could ever dislike anything they had written.

"The trouble with the One Star Club is that it doesn't exist. And even if it did, there's no reason to believe that Winnie or Teena were members. So we keep coming back to the question of why Winnie was killed. Why? She seemed perfectly nice. It was a senseless killing, and yet it all seemed to have been planned out so carefully."

"Why do you say it was planned, m'dear? Couldn't it have been an opportunistic attack?"

"The polls were rigged to bring Winnie here. None of the organizing committee remembered voting for her piece of fiction."

"Well blow me down. I thought I'd lost my mind!" Cerys looked round at her friends. "Do none of you remember? It's not just me?"

"So who stood to gain from her death? Her husband, maybe. But he was in another country. Her elderly relatives in Milton Keynes. But they're elderly. And they were in Milton Keynes."

She looked for confirmation to Det. James, in position at the door. He nodded.

"Then there was Maggie, of course—with Winnie and Teena out of the way, she was the clear winner in the online fiction competition."

"Ooh yes!" Everyone in the room wanted it to be Maggie.

"But that's not a very strong reason. There was no financial reward, and besides, she was already a winner. But the members of the RWGB made a financial gain. There was a terrific boost to book sales at the conference after Winnie's death—they even had to bring in a local bookseller specially, to sell books to the people who'd turned up for the vigil. There was renewed press interest in the RWGB, which is suffering from dwindling membership. It struggles to get noticed in comparison to some other associations for romance writers. So, we're back to the organizing committee again."

"You don't know who did it, do you?" Polly spoke gently and kindly. "Come on, Emily. There's no shame in admitting it. It's been an interesting exercise. But maybe we should move on and leave the investigation to the police."

"I do know. I'll tell you how I know. It's because of the anomalies. And it's because of the smokers and the litter. And it's because of the job I was doing before this one, where I used to wait for ages to get in the elevator, and then when I got in, no one would ever press the button for me because they were so rude and self-involved. So I used to wish that I had my own private elevator to take me up and down between the floors. And here in the hotel, the guest elevators are even slower. And you know what I realized? The killer was using the service elevator like a private elevator. And that's important because it's all about timings and alibis. And that's another reason I know who did it—the alibis. But first I'll tell you about the anomalies, shall I?"

"OK," said Det. James from the back of the room. "Be great if you could get this over and done with before my boss arrives."

"The poisoning's the big one. Two murders that fit with each other, and then there's an attempted poisoning of Polly with a chocolate. I mean, why? And then there's this weird phone call I got from Winnie, speaking in a Southern accent. Except it wasn't Winnie because she was already dead. And there was the way that nobody really seemed to care about what happened to Teena because it had all already happened to Winnie. But the weirdest one, the one that's the key to it all, is what the doctor said to me in Polly's room when she came to check her over after Polly'd been sick."

"Maybe it wasn't a real doctor?" said Cerys, getting into the spirit of it. "Did you check?"

Nik called from the back of the room: "It was our usual doctor. I sent her up there myself."

Polly shrugged and blushed. "It was all rather embarrassing, really. She said I was having a panic attack."

"The doctor got angry with me. She said that you mustn't administer the antidote to a patient without knowing for sure if they've been poisoned, because it could be really dangerous. That was the anomaly. The doctor talking about the antidote."

"The doctor did it?" said Cerys, puzzled. "Are you sure, love?"

"The doctor?" the buzz went up around the room. "Did she say the doctor? The doctor did it!"

"*It wasn't the doctor!*" Emily had to raise her voice to make herself heard. "It was Polly."

CHAPTER EIGHTEEN
THE HOW AND WHY

"This wasn't about Winnie at all. Teena was the main target. She lived in a village in Buckinghamshire, not far from Polly. Like lots of bloggers, she liked blogging so much that she had more than one blog. She reviewed books at TeeandBooks.com. But she also wrote about local news at the Buckinghamshire Bugle. Teena was proud of being a 'citizen journalist,' covering everything from restaurant reviews to village fetes, from cricket matches to campaigns against accident blackspots, and so on. I was reading her blog just now, before I came down here. She had rather an unfortunate manner in person, but she was articulate and persuasive when she wrote online. She was vehemently in favor of renewable energy and had got the whole village behind her. One of the things she campaigned for was a wind farm. Wind farms...well one of the problems with them is that birds fly into their rotary blades and get shredded. Polly's husband had just taken over a bird sanctuary in the area."

"The swannery!"

Polly was unmoved. She certainly wasn't about to admit to murder. "We look after swans there, yes. All sorts of birds. Pete's a vet. He likes taking in broken and injured birds—if they've swallowed fishing tackle or been covered in oil in an oil spill, that sort of thing."

"Aww," said several people in the room.

"He's a decent man. Yes."

But Emily wasn't about to get distracted. "He was fighting, and losing, a campaign against the wind farm. Polly uses her maiden name on her books so as not to confuse her fans, so I doubt Teena had any idea that her favorite novelist's husband was involved."

"But you did!" said Dr. Muriel. "Clever girl!"

"Look, I wouldn't have got this, I don't suppose," said Emily self-deprecatingly, as if they were discussing the answers to a difficult pub quiz, "if I hadn't stood in the Brunswick room and looked at those blogs scrolling down the screen in tribute to Winnie. I wondered—I hoped—there'd be some kind of message from Teena since it was the last thing she did before she died. There *was* a message, though she didn't leave it deliberately. She'd set up the computer to grab information from all the blogs written by Winnie's friends around the world and display them, and she included both of hers."

"The universe always finds a way to get that message across, babes."

"Darling, couldn't Polly—and I do think you'll find you've got a bit mixed up here and you'll find she's entirely innocent, but I'm going to play along anyway—couldn't Polly just have campaigned against the wind farm instead of killing two people and poisoning herself?"

"I'm guessing it's something to do with her wanting to stand as a Member of Parliament. A campaign like that would be too controversial. She'd never get elected."

Polly gave a relaxed, slightly condescending smile, like a cowboy watching a duchess learning to use a lasso. "The voters are not notably keener on murderers than they are on anti-wind-farm campaigners."

"But you thought you'd get away with murder," said Emily. "The voters weren't supposed to know what you'd done. You couldn't have campaigned against the wind farm in secret."

"Polly does care about her birds," said Cerys. "Remember that business with the goose at the RWGB Christmas dinner?"

"We've had the why, m'dear. Shall we get onto the how?"

"Polly invited Winnie to go up to the roof terrace to smoke a cigarette. What an honor! Her heroine offering her a cigarette, and inviting her to hide round the back of the bar like a schoolgirl, while they chatted about writing and indulged their sneaky habit."

"Aha!"

"But Polly had doctored all the cigarettes in the packet. Winnie takes one. Polly lights it for her. Winnie takes one puff and gets dizzy. Polly pushes her over the fence, and Winnie lands in the bins below and breaks her neck. Polly didn't expect the body to be found for an hour or two. So she calls and talks to me, pretending to be Winnie, to give herself an alibi."

Det. James called out, "Why the ridiculous accent?"

"To cause more confusion. Maybe she thought she'd shift suspicion to whoever took the call—originally she asked for Morgana, but she ended up speaking to me—if we claimed to have spoken to someone who didn't speak like Winnie at all. Or more likely she wanted to establish the person on the other end of the line as an unreliable witness, in case the timing of the call didn't quite fit with her alibi. But anyway she called. And then she came down to the ground floor."

"Where she proceeded to move the body?"

"No, that's just it. She wanted the body to be found where it fell, so it would look like an accident. And then Teena's death would follow after, with less scrutiny, as an also-ran. But someone else moved Winnie's body and sparked a murder inquiry. I don't suppose we'll ever know who."

Emily avoided looking at Nik.

"So that's the smoking. Now the litter. When I first met Polly, she had a long stub of a cigarette in her hand. It was the first of only two times I ever saw her bother to pick up a cigarette butt. The second was just after Teena's death. As Winnie—and, later, Teena—went sailing over the edge of the roof terrace, they'd dropped the cigarette they'd been holding into the courtyard below. Polly wasn't tidying her litter. She was removing evidence. See, that's where what the doctor said about the antidote comes in. I looked it up online—"

"Isn't that cheating?" asked Dr. Muriel. "I tell my students not to google anything."

"Well, I didn't have time to go to the British Library. So I looked it up online and the antidote to cyanide poisoning—or one of them, anyway—is amyl nitrite. It's sold legally, over the counter, as a muscle relaxant. Popular in nightclubs as a legal high. You can sniff it or you can dip a cigarette into it and inhale it that way. Of course, if you didn't have cyanide poisoning and you weren't used to doing drugs in nightclubs, you'd be knocked half sideways if someone took you up on a roof and offered you a cigarette that had been dipped in the stuff. Dizziness, low blood pressure, fainting. While you were dealing with that, two hands in the middle of your chest, whoosh!"

"I didn't think you went clubbing, Emily," said Polly, mildly.

"I don't. But I know what people get up to when they go. Besides, you click on one link on the Internet, it take you to another one, and another. I had all the information I needed about amyl nitrite—and more—after five minutes of searching on the computer in Nik's office."

Morgana's hand went to the pompom on her hat, and she squeezed it a few times, like a stress ball. "Darling, you don't need to tell anyone in this room. We're all convinced we could write ten books a year if we didn't spend our valuable writing time looking at the Internet."

All the authors laughed at that, some more bitterly than others.

Emily addressed Polly directly: "You used to do a lot of clubbing when you were younger, didn't you say?"

"I've made no secret of it. I've talked about it on Twitter. But I never did poppers."

"Yes! Poppers. That's what it's called in club culture. Thank you. I think the doctor must have seen a bottle of it on the dressing table in your room. I don't know for sure but…"

Emily looked over at Rory. He nodded. "I'll get the boys on it."

"But why all that nonsense about the poisoning in the first place?" Dr. Muriel banged her cane on the ground at the stupidity of it.

"It would give Polly another murder method if she needed it. So if she couldn't get Teena up to the roof to push her off, she could put poison in her food later that night or at breakfast, or slip something into her drink, and no one would suspect her because she'd also been a victim. There was no real rush, just so long as it happened that weekend and seemed to be connected to Winnie's death, and was overshadowed by it."

Emily looked over at Det. James, who tapped his watch to get her to hurry up and finish. A uniformed officer now stood by his side.

"The timing's all wrong for Teena's death," said Cerys. "How could Polly get up to the roof and back down again to the bins where you found her? You're not saying she can fly like her precious birds?"

"When she turned up to help me pack the gift bags, she arrived in the service elevator. And that's how she traveled all weekend. While the rest of us would wait for ages to travel from floor to floor in the guest elevator, she went the quick way. I think, once the CCTV pictures are checked, the timings'll fit."

"So, love, help me out here? Polly rigged the vote?"

"I don't know if Polly rigged it or…" Emily avoided looking at Morgana. "Or someone else. But as soon as they accepted the invitation to come here, Teena's and Winnie's deaths were inevitable. Teena because of her campaign in the Buckinghamshire Bugle. And Winnie because she was visiting from a foreign country, and that made her interesting. Her death would seem like the focus for the story, instead of a footnote."

Maggie piped up. "Can I just say, about the murders, that I don't think Polly did it?"

No one took any notice of her, so she added, "And also, she's my favorite novelist." At which point half the room wished (and then felt guilty, and tried to unwish it) that Polly had done a more thorough job and finished off all three of them.

"So anyway, that's it." Too late, Emily realized she should have prepared a more rousing conclusion.

"A very, very good story," Polly drawled. She didn't look fazed by it at all. "Most people here wish they could work up such a detailed story from such scant notes."

"You're against the wind farm, are you, Poll?" Cerys was very keen to get the details right.

"I believe there are better ways of getting sustainable energy than setting up giant mincing machines that chop birds out of the sky. But that doesn't mean I'm guilty of murder."

The uniformed officer, with a fine sense of drama, now stepped forward and held up a clear plastic bag containing a small brown bottle. "Maybe this does. Amyl nitrite. Colloquially known as poppers. Found on Miss Penham's dressing table."

The room responded appreciatively: "Ooh!"

Morgana stood up. "I think that's as good a point as any to break for coffee, don't you? Big round of applause for Emily Castles, who led such an interesting session this morning. On behalf of the Romance Writers of Great Britain, thank you, Emily."

Everyone applauded, and then surged out of the room for coffee, cake and gossip.

While the uniformed officer arrested Polly Penham and read her her rights, Rory James came up to Emily and gave her a big smile. "Well done, Emily. Look, when I'm done with my paperwork, do you fancy going for a drink?"

A sweet, dimpled smile. "Thanks. But I think I've had enough romance for one weekend."

Zena walked past with Cerys, a note of awe in her voice: "That doll melting, it was an accident, yeah? But it shows it works. You don't mess with the altar. Cause today, you gotta admit it, that girl got *burned*."

Emily caught up with Dr. Muriel at the door to the Montagu room where she had been detained by Nik Kovacevic. He said, "About the One Star Club—"

"Nik, it doesn't exist."

"Yes, but if one wanted to start such a thing up. Where would one advertise for members, do you think?"

"Ha!" said Dr. Muriel, taking Emily's arm and walking out of the door. "Ha-ha."

"You know," said Emily to her friend. "When you asked me to lead the session this morning, I thought it was one of your daft experiments."

"Indeed. Of course it was. This one worked astoundingly well, though. Eh? Eh?"

Dr. Muriel laughed her dirty laugh as they walked to where the coffee and cake had been set up.

Nik Kovacevic walked past them back to his office, a brilliant idea forming in his head about a secret society he planned to set up. As a chef walked past them in the other direction, Emily could have sworn she heard someone singing, very quietly, yet mockingly: "Heigh-ho!"

Upstairs in her room, Maggie Tambling was already on the third paragraph of a fluently written, witty blog post that would eventually run to more than two thousand words. It would become the most popular post on her already-popular Tamble with Me at Your Own Risk! blog, referenced by the *Guardian* books blog, linked to by bloggers, spoofed by hipsters, quoted on Twitter by Stephen Fry and Neil Gaiman, and earning Maggie the first nomination for a nonprint journalist for the irreverent Stabbies Awards for reviewers who, in the words of the organizers, "eviscerate the pretensions of authors and their acolytes." The award would be won by a journalist from the *New York Times*: her reviews were so poisonous, so her colleagues quipped, that she kept an antidote by her computer, in case her words should ever come back to bite her. But Maggie was proud, as she had been in the inaugural and never-to-be-repeated RWGB short fiction competition, to be among the top three.

The title of Maggie's blog post was "Romance Writers Get Busy: The Hate, the Hats and a Helluva Way to Die."

ACKNOWLEDGMENTS

Thank you to Andy Bartlett, Jacque Ben-Zekry and the wonderful team at Thomas & Mercer. I'm grateful to everyone who has been involved in the production, design and marketing of this book.

Thanks also to my lovely new agent, David Hale Smith at Ink-Well Management.

I have a friend called Brenda Castles, and she has a sister called Emily. Emily and I have never met, but I liked her name enough to borrow it for the main character in my mystery series, with her permission. Thanks to the Castles family. I hope your mam likes the book, Emily.

Thank you to Al Kunz and Lauren Smith, who read the manuscript before publication.

Lauren has read every book and every play I have ever written and given me useful notes on all of them. She has never complained about this. I borrowed Lauren's sweet nature, her dimples and her freckles for my descriptions of Emily in the book. Thanks for being my inspiration and my joy, Lauren.

Thanks to my parents for your love and support. Thanks also to my extended family and my friends.

I went to Bouchercon last year for the first time. Thanks to everyone who made me laugh and made me feel so welcome, and to Lauren Henderson, who introduced me to many of you.

Still with me? Thank you for reading *Invitation to Die*. I hope you enjoyed the book.

ABOUT THE AUTHOR

Helen Smith is a novelist and playwright who lives in London. In addition to the Emily Castles mysteries, she is the author of *Alison Wonderland, Being Light* and *The Miracle Inspector*.

Kindle *Serials*

This book was originally released in episodes as a Kindle Serial. Kindle Serials launched in 2012 as a new way to experience serialized books. Kindle Serials allow readers to enjoy the story as the author creates it, purchasing once and receiving all existing episodes immediately, followed by future episodes as they are published. To find out more about Kindle Serials and to see the current selection of Serials titles, visit www.amazon.com/kindleserials.